GW00383325

THE TROUBLE AT WAKELEY COURT

An Angela Marchmont Mystery Book 8

CLARA BENSON

MOUNT STREET PRESS

© 2015 Clara Benson
All rights reserved

ISBN: 978-1-913355-26-5

The right of Clara Benson to be identified as the author of this work
has been asserted by her in accordance with the Copyright, Designs and
Patents Act, 1988

The characters and events portrayed in this book are fictitious. Any
similarity to real persons, living or dead, is coincidental and not
intended by the author

This book is sold subject to the condition that it shall not, by way of
trade or otherwise, be lent, resold, hired out, or otherwise circulated
without the publisher's prior consent in any form of binding or cover
other than that in which it is published and without a similar condition
including this condition being imposed upon the subsequent purchaser

clarabenson.com

The Trouble at Wakeley Court

When the Grand Duke of Morania learns of a plot to assassinate him, he sends his daughter Princess Irina to school in England, out of harm's way. British Intelligence scent trouble and ask Angela Marchmont to investigate. But dark forces are at work, and when the Princess disappears in mysterious circumstances Angela must race against time to find her, before the throne falls and Morania is plunged into revolution—or war.

Chapter One

FEODOR, Grand Duke of Morania, stood at the window of his palace and gazed down thoughtfully into the square below. From his vantage point he could see the people scurrying about through the streets of the capital city, Vorgorod, and as always at such times he took a moment to reflect upon the privilege that had bestowed upon him the rulership of such a proud, industrious nation. The Grand Duke was not a man who took things for granted. He had worked hard to bring peace and prosperity to his people, and he took a quiet satisfaction in the state of things at present, which was in no small measure due to his own hard work and dedication. It was he who had striven to bring industrial methods to this largely agrarian country, despite some natural resistance on the part of the populace, who had done things the same way for centuries and found nothing to criticize in the *status quo*. It was he who had insisted that every male citizen be given the vote regardless of his wealth or position in society. This in particular had required the utmost diplomacy and finesse, but he had carried it off in the end. Little did his opponents know that the Grand Duke had some vague thought of one day extending the franchise to women, too—although he judged it politic to remain silent on this subject at present, since he was well aware that to introduce too much change at once would be unwise. Still, he relished the thought of the tasks that lay ahead of him in his quest to transform Morania into a modern nation and make it a power to be reckoned with on the international stage. There was still much to be done, but he was a determined man, and had no doubt that he would succeed in the end.

He turned away from the window and sat down at his enormous, carved desk. He might have had one of the larger chambers in which to conduct his daily business, but he had broken with tradition, instead preferring to carry out the ordinary duties of state in a smaller, more comfortable, less imposing side-room. As he took his seat, a lackey hastened forth and respectfully handed him some papers.

'The preliminary agreement from Krovodar, sire,' said the lackey.

The Grand Duke read through the pages with care, and shook his head.

'This is not correct,' he said. 'It was all agreed quite clearly, but I see a sentence has been added to the end of the document which changes the meaning of the first paragraph entirely. It was most likely an error on their part.' His face was non-committal, for he was a statesman through and through and was never unguarded enough to reveal his true thoughts before his inferiors. 'Have the Krovodanian ambassador called in,' he went on. 'Let us see what he makes of it.'

'At once, sire,' said the lackey.

The Grand Duke then turned his attention to the other documents in the pile and occupied himself with mundane matters of policy until he was interrupted by the entrance of another man for whom all the servants in the room stood to attention. This man was some years younger than the Grand Duke, but appeared to be a person of some importance. He approached the desk, bowed, and addressed the older man with a combination of respect and familiarity.

'Good morning, Paul,' said the Grand Duke. 'How goes it?'

'Good morning, *Velkji Knaz*,' said the newcomer. His expression was serious.

The Grand Duke looked at him keenly.

'There is something, I can see,' he said. 'Bad news, I imagine. You had better tell me at once.'

Paul, Count of Vorgorod and second minister in the Moranian government, smiled ruefully.

'It is impossible to keep anything from you,' he said. 'Yes, there is something. This morning I had word from Everich. He is very worried.'

'It is his job to be worried,' said the Grand Duke. 'That is what we pay him for—to do our worrying for us and spare us the trouble.'

'I am afraid it is no laughing matter,' said Count Paul soberly. He glanced about him. 'Leave us,' he said to the various attendants who stood about in the chamber.

The Grand Duke nodded and they all went out obediently. Then he turned back to Count Paul and raised his eyebrows.

'My dear boy, this must be serious indeed,' he said. 'What did Everich have to say for himself? Are we having trouble with the revolutionaries again?'

'No,' said Count Paul. 'The threat is more deadly than that. This one comes from Krovodar, and is nothing less than a plot to assassinate you and—I am afraid—Princess Irina.'

The Grand Duke was surprised. He frowned.

'Are you quite certain of this?' he said.

'Oh, yes,' said the other. 'The intelligence comes from an impeccable source.'

'I see,' said the Grand Duke. 'That is rather tiresome. Still, is it worthy of our attention? Such a plot cannot come from on high, given our present relations with Krovodar. Surely it is a mere nothing which can be dealt with by them. I assume they are aware of the matter?'

Count Paul looked even more sober.

'I regret to say that you are mistaken,' he said. 'Everich has evidence that the plot was not only approved at the highest level, but in fact originated from there.'

The Grand Duke stared.

'Impossible!' he exclaimed.

'Indeed, that is what I should have said myself until this morning,' said Count Paul. 'It is all thanks to your efforts that we have been on such polite terms with Krovodar for the past ten years. However, it seems that some elements in the government are tiring of the *détente* and have begun to talk about annexing Iszbicka. Their election was a close-run thing, of course, and the government's position is weak, and so they are anxious to demonstrate their strength. What better way to do that than by directing attention away from the poverty of their people and towards the old enemy? Already there are rumblings in the street that Morania has no right to Iszbicka, and that the Krovodanians who live there must be reunited with their mother country. I am very much afraid that your name is being mentioned as the one responsible for having taken the territory from Krovodar in the first place.'

'That is nonsense, of course,' said the Grand Duke. 'The Krovodanians have not ruled over Iszbicka since the fifteenth century. I don't deny that my forebears took it from them five hundred years ago, but of course I had nothing to do with it myself. And they have made no formal claim to the place since 1894, if my memory serves me correctly. They like to bring up the subject on official occasions, but we all nod and smile politely and agree that perhaps we will begin talks on the matter in the next few years, and the conversation turns to other things.'

'It appears, then, that feelings on the subject are stronger than we thought,' said Count Paul.

The Grand Duke picked up the paper which he had refused to sign earlier. It was an agreement allowing Krovodar certain rights to exploit copper deposits in the region of Iszbicka, close to the Krovodanian border. The sentence which had been added at the end could, if read in a certain way, be interpreted as giving Krovodar far more rights than had been originally agreed. It might easily have been put there by mistake, but if what Count Paul said was true then the thing took on an altogether different aspect.

'But Paul, why have I heard nothing of this before?' said the Grand Duke suddenly. 'If things have reached the point at which another country is planning to have me and my daughter assassinated, then do not you think I ought to have been informed of the matter earlier?'

'Believe me, sire, you should have been, had we been aware of it,' said Count Paul. 'But Everich says the secrecy surrounding the plot has been so complete that only now have his spies been able to find out anything about it. There were rumours of Krovodar's discontent a few months ago, but they were no more than the usual sort of thing—nothing we have not heard before, given that relations between our two countries have never been exactly warm.'

'No,' agreed the Grand Duke. 'The peace has always been an uneasy one, but I have worked hard to maintain it, and it pains me now to hear that it may all have been for nothing. What do they hope to achieve by my death? It is a bold move, and there are surely better ways for them to get what they want.'

'I think the intention is to create a vacuum of sorts. Princess Irina is the last of the royal Ivanoveti line, and if both of you can be put out of the way at once, Krovodar will have the opportunity to seize Iszbicka—and most likely the rest of Morania if it chooses—even before all your second and third cousins have had time to return from exile and begin squabbling over the throne.'

'It is a pity you cannot inherit, Paul,' said the Grand Duke. 'I do not blame my cousin for marrying your mother, for she was a delightful woman in every way, but the marriage came with many sacrifices. The people of Morania have never looked kindly upon morganatic alliances. They are not especially happy at the idea of a woman's taking the throne either, but in this they have no choice, since Irina is my only child and all my distant relations are so eminently unsuitable. Still, I shall rely upon you to provide Irina with counsel and support when the time comes for her to take my place.'

'I shall do it with pleasure, but let us hope that that day is far in the future,' said the Count.

'I entirely agree with you,' said the Grand Duke dryly. 'I am not ready to depart this earth *quite* yet, and if anything can keep me alive, the thought of a fifteen-year-old girl's inheriting the throne ought to do it. She has all the intelligence and at least some of the sense of her mother, and I have no doubt that one day she will rule wisely—especially if we can find a suitable husband for her —but she is by no means ready yet, nor will she be for many years. She must finish her education first.'

'Then you are still determined to send her to England?'

'Yes. She will go to school. It will do her good to mix with other girls again, and I have no doubt that she will be happy to return to England. She has spent too long alone here in the palace since the death of her mother, and I am certain the change will do her good. She will be sixteen soon, and will have to start taking on some official duties, so it will be good for her to have a little freedom before it all begins. And naturally, if there really is a threat to her life as you say, then it is of the utmost importance that she be sent away from the danger.'

'Where does she go?'

'To a school called Wakeley Court,' said the Grand Duke. 'It is in Norfolk, in a very healthy spot not far from the sea. I have been impressed with what I hear of the place, and it comes highly recommended. There all the girls are treated equally, and no distinctions are made. Irina has been taught well and is not one to give herself airs, but it is a lesson that cannot be learned often enough. To rule a country well one must understand humility.'

'She is a good girl,' said Count Paul with a smile. 'I have no doubt that she will do very well at school. But sire, shall you warn her of the threat to her life? Perhaps it would be better not to mention it, or she might become fearful.'

The Grand Duke reflected for a moment.

'No, I think it will be better to tell her,' he said. 'Such threats are unavoidable in our position, I regret to say, and if she knows of the danger then she can look out for it and help herself if necessary. She is old enough to understand, and I would not have her live in ignorance on such an important matter.'

'But she will be so out of the way in Norfolk,' said Count Paul. 'Surely there is no danger so far from home.'

'One never knows,' replied the Grand Duke. 'At any

rate, I am glad I had not yet mentioned the plan to anybody, for it will be better to keep it as secret as possible. The fewer people who know, the better.'

'That is true enough,' agreed the Count. 'But sire, you must not forget that Irina is not the only one in danger. What ought we to do about the threat to *your* life? We must arrange protection for you. I shall see to it myself personally.'

'We will talk about it later,' said the Grand Duke with a wave of the hand. 'You have official duties to see to this morning, as do I. But first, I should like to speak to Irina. Kindly have her summoned.'

Count Paul bowed and accepted his dismissal. As he waited for his daughter to answer the summons, the Grand Duke stood by the window, deep in thought. In due course Princess Irina presented herself before her father and they exchanged the usual courtesies. They spoke in English, as they were accustomed to do—partly because it was the language Irina had spoken from a child and partly because they preferred not to allow the servants to overhear all their private business.

'Is it about school?' said Irina. 'When am I to go?'

'Soon,' said her father. 'Next week, if it can be arranged.'

Her rather solemn face lit up.

'How marvellous!' she said. 'It seems an age since I was in England. I *have* missed it so.'

'Yes,' said the Grand Duke. 'I thought you would be pleased. I ought to have sent you a year ago, but I am a selfish old man and did not like the idea of being parted from you.'

'You're not selfish at all,' she said. 'I shall miss you too, but I'll write often so you won't *really* be parted from me. And of course I'll be back for the holidays.'

The Grand Duke regarded his daughter with a smile. How quickly she had grown up! It seemed only yesterday that he had been presented with the tiny, mewling thing and had stifled his disappointment on finding that she was not the son he had wanted. But she had quickly worked her way into his affections and ever since then she had been the light and the pride of his life. Naturally, a son would have been better for the future of Morania, but the Grand Duke was not one to dwell on what could not be helped. Under his tutelage, Princess Irina would come to understand the duties of state and would one day rule the country in his stead. Until then, however, she had many things to learn—of which one was an unfortunate fact about the position of royalty.

'Come to the window, my child,' he said. 'I have something of importance to tell you and it is better not to be overheard, even if they don't understand what we are saying.'

Irina glanced at the attendants and did as she was bid.

'What is it?' she said.

'It is not an easy matter of which to speak to a young girl,' he said, 'but I believe it is important that you know, for it affects you directly. I have heard this morning that some bad men intend to make an attempt on my life—and, I am afraid, yours too.'

'Oh!' said Irina. 'Who wants to kill us?'

'The Krovodanians. It appears they are not as well-disposed towards us as they would have us believe,' said the Grand Duke dryly.

'Is it because of Iszbicka?' said Irina. 'They want it back, don't they? That's where the copper mines are. They're jolly valuable, I've heard.'

'That is part of the reason,' replied her father. He was surprised and not a little impressed at her knowledge, for he had not believed her to take much interest in these things. 'Another part of it has to do with internal politics in Krovodar. Our deaths would help make their government more popular.'

'I understand,' said Irina. 'Yes, it would distract attention from their own problems pretty neatly, wouldn't it?' A thought struck her. 'Who told you about it?'

'Paul, just now,' said the Grand Duke.

'Oh, Paul. Then it must be true. Had it been anyone else I should have suspected it was just a ploy to make you afraid.'

'What do you mean?' he said, taken aback. 'A ploy by whom?'

'Why, your exiled cousins, of course. You told me yourself that they have half the ministers in Vorgorod in their pay. You know how they all lick their lips at the thought of marrying me and getting their hands on the throne once you're gone.'

'I did tell you that, it is true,' said the Grand Duke, thinking to himself that perhaps he ought to be more careful about what he told his daughter in future, since she seemed to absorb such information with great efficiency. He had idly mentioned his suspicions about his ministers when the two of them were alone, but had not supposed that she was listening with great attention. 'But I don't see how it would benefit them to tell me they want me dead.'

'Nor do I,' said Irina. 'It just occurred to me that that sort of silly intrigue would be just like them.'

'At any rate, that is beside the point,' said the Grand Duke. 'I have told you all this because you are an intelligent girl and old enough to take some responsibility for protecting yourself. You will be going to school next week, and I am glad of it, for it will put you out of reach of those who wish you harm. Few people know about it, and you must keep it quiet yourself now that we know of this plot.'

'I will,' said Irina. 'I promise I won't breathe a word to anyone.'

'Good,' said her father. 'I confess it will be a relief to me to get you safely out of the way, and I think that if we take one or two extra precautions, then we shall do very well. I am glad that your mother and I made the decision to shield you from the public gaze until you were old enough to assume royal duties, for that means you are not recognizable to most people, which is very helpful to us in the present instance.'

'That's true enough,' said Irina. 'Nobody knows who I am, so with any luck I ought to be perfectly safe.'

'Let us hope so,' said the Grand Duke.

'I can't wait to go to school,' said Irina happily. 'It's going to be such fun.'

Chapter Two

'So I am afraid, Mrs. Marchmont, that we will no longer be able to keep her,' said Miss Bell. 'Barbara is a decent girl at heart, but there is a streak of disobedience and waywardness in her that we have been unable to overcome. Perhaps at another school she will do better.'

Angela Marchmont sat in Miss Bell's study, in one of the comfortable chairs reserved for parents and visitors, and gazed out of the handsome arched window and across the lawns down to the lake, where a number of girls were taking advantage of an unusually warm spell of weather to sit on the grass reading quietly or talking. One or two of them were tossing a ball about idly. The scene was very wholesome.

Miss Bell was still speaking.

'As you know, Barbara was given several warnings last year about her behaviour, and I had hoped that the long summer break would have given her time to mature a little, and reflect on her shortcomings. However, I regret to say that the passage of time appears to have made no difference. Her guardians, the Ellises, are abroad at present, of course, which is why I called you. I understand they will not be back until early in the new year.'

'No,' said Angela, rousing herself. 'They won't—' Here she bit back an 'unfortunately,' since she did not wish to sound uncaring.

She looked at Miss Bell. The headmistress of Wakeley Court school was an imposing woman, with an impressive bosom and an arrangement of hair which seemed to have been created by the sculptor's art rather than a brush and comb. Her manner was firm, but not unsympathetic. Angela recognized the type, having met with similar during her own school years: unimaginative and conventional, but a natural leader who saw everything, stood no nonsense and was admired for it. No doubt Miss Bell was loved and respected by all her girls, but that was of little comfort in the present situation. Mrs. Marchmont was very fond of her god-daughter, but was thrown into a panic at the idea of having to find another school which would accept Barbara at such short notice, after her expulsion from this one in disgrace. Angela had several imminent engagements which it would be difficult to put off, including a half-promised trip to Paris with some friends, and the thought of having to bring along an unruly fourteen-year-old while the search for a new school went on did not appeal. One could hardly enjoy oneself freely in such circumstances, since one would be continually aware of the need to set a good example. Not that one *deliberately* set out to misbe-have, naturally, but one's liberty of action would be severely curtailed. No: another school would have to be found, and quickly.

But how exactly *did* one go about selecting a school? Such decisions had always been left to Nina and Gerald in the past. Barbara had already moved once, having been unhappy at her previous place near London. This one,

Wakeley Court, was supposed to be one of the best girls' schools in the country, turning out well-educated, well-balanced, confident young ladies, and for a while it had seemed the perfect choice for Barbara, who was an intelligent child but easily bored. Here, she would be given interesting lessons, kept busy and, it was hoped, learn to suppress her natural inclination to get up to mischief. For the first term, indeed, it had looked as though the move had been a success. No reports had been received of any misbehaviour, and to judge from her occasional scrawled letters, Barbara had settled in nicely and was enjoying herself. Soon enough, however, she had fallen back into her old ways, and had begun to get into trouble. She was not a wicked child, but she was afflicted with an insatiable curiosity and an unfortunate inability to think through the consequences of her actions. She was also unable to resist a dare—a fact of which her school-mates were well aware and took full advantage for their own entertainment. Again and again she promised faithfully to turn over a new leaf, but she found it so dreadfully hard to do what she ought, and sooner or later she inevitably got into some scrape or other.

'What exactly did Barbara do?' said Angela. 'Your letter hinted at something rather terrible but gave no details. I confess it frightened me a little.'

'Several things,' said Miss Bell. 'I have it all here in the black mark book.'

She picked up the book in question and opened it. Angela craned her neck, trying to read upside down. The page had a long list of entries, and Angela thought she could read the name Barbara in several of them.

'Just to take an example at random,' the headmistress continued, 'shortly after term began she embarrassed one of the trustees by pretending to mistake him for a well-known film-actor and requesting his autograph in front of a group of visiting parents.'

'Perhaps that was a genuine mistake,' said Angela, although she was certain it was not, as it sounded just the sort of thing Barbara would do.

'That is possible,' conceded Miss Bell, 'although the gentleman in question is not exactly—how shall I put it?—possessed of the type of appearance which one would normally associate with film-actors. In addition, there was an unusually large number of girls present at the time, which leads me to suspect that the thing was arranged in advance. A week after that, Barbara was caught on the roof—which is strictly out of bounds—dropping eggs into the Quad. She claimed to be reproducing Galileo's experiments with falling objects, but of course that is nonsense. Even if it were true, a more suitable way of doing it could have been found. I fear Mr. Penkridge's coat was quite ruined—although to give her credit, Barbara was genuinely contrite and offered to pay for a new one.'

'I see,' said Angela.

'I shall not give you the whole list of black marks as we have not the time, and it must be said that most of them are too minor to mention, but they all add up to a pattern of most unladylike and rebellious behaviour—not at all what we expect of girls at Wakeley Court. Some of them are too serious to overlook, however, and are the reason for which I have been forced to reconsider Barbara's continuing as a pupil here.' Miss Bell paused impressively. 'I regret to have to tell you, Mrs. Marchmont, that last week we discovered that Barbara had been—I believe the term is "*running a book.*"'

'Running a book?' said Angela. 'Do you mean taking bets? On the horses, and suchlike?'

'Not exactly,' said Miss Bell. 'It appears the girls have

invented a game in which they attempt to induce the teachers to say a particular word by the end of the lesson, by leading the conversation in an artful manner. They began with Miss Devlin, who has an unfortunate speech impediment which prevents her from saying the letter R correctly. It seems that some of the girls find it funny to trick her into saying words which contain that very letter. Take a look at this.'

She picked up a notebook from her desk and handed it to Angela, who raised her eyebrows and took it. On the front cover the words, 'Barbara Wells—private,' were printed in large capital letters. Inside, each page was divided neatly into lines and columns, all filled with what looked like code—dates, numbers and scribbled letters in different coloured inks, with the occasional recognizable name or word.

'As you can see,' went on Miss Bell, indicating with a pencil, 'in the first week they tried to make Miss Devlin say the word "rarity," and it appears they were successful in their attempt.'

Angela saw the neat tick, and the note, 'Paid, I. C.' next to it.

'What is I. C.?' she said.

'I believe it refers to Isabel Chambers, a class-mate of Barbara's,' said Miss Bell.

'Ah, yes,' said Angela. 'Then this column of initials is a record of the—er—punters.' She examined the page with interest. 'Goodness,' she said. 'I had no idea she had such a good grasp of betting odds. Why, look at the calculations in the margin here. I can't find a single mistake.'

'I have no complaints about Barbara's arithmetical ability,' said Miss Bell, throwing Angela an odd look. 'That is not the point, however. You must admit that this prank and the planning which has gone into it indicate a certain perversity of mind, to say the very least. As you can see, as the weeks went on, they expanded the game to include the rest of the teachers, and increased the difficulty of the challenge by making the words to be drawn from them ever more outlandish.'

'So I see,' said Angela. 'Look—someone called M. B. managed to get Miss Finch to say "fandango," "canoodle" and "interfenestration" all in one lesson. That's rather impressive. I see no one has managed "anencephalous" or "platitudinarianism" yet, though. Or "callipygian,"' she added.

'I should think not,' said Miss Bell primly. She had a slight suspicion that Mrs. Marchmont was not taking the conversation as seriously as she ought, and gave a cough. 'That is the least of it, however. If you turn to the back of the book, you will see another set of figures, under the heading "Mr. Wilde." Mr. Wilde is the vicar who gives most of the Sunday services in our school chapel here. Unfortunately for him, he suffers from a tendency to sneeze in the presence of dust, and despite our best efforts the chapel seems to bring on frequent and severe attacks of this nature. According to the book, Barbara has also been accepting bets on the number of times Mr. Wilde will sneeze during any given sermon. Shameful though it is, it appears that this is a particularly popular game with the girls, for the list of participants is rather long. I am sure I need not say that attention to religion is something that we take with the utmost seriousness here, Mrs. Marchmont, and I cannot have any of our girls showing such flagrant disrespect for its observance during periods of worship. As the ringleader, Barbara must take much of the blame for this.'

'Dear me, quite,' said Angela, arranging her face into what she hoped was a suitably solemn expression. 'It is most worrying. Still, I am relieved to hear that her transgressions appear to be a case of excessively high spirits, rather than anything truly wicked. I should hate to think that she had done anything bad-natured. At least she has not hurt anybody.'

'Unfortunately, I am rather afraid she has,' said Miss Bell. 'That is the worst of it. I should never have thought her to be the type of girl to harm someone maliciously, but two days ago I regret to say she was caught in the act of shoving a fellow pupil against a wall. The same pupil had earlier complained that Barbara deliberately whacked her on the leg with a hockey stick, although Barbara claimed it was an accident. I need not say that we do *not* tolerate such disgraceful behaviour at Wakeley Court. We do not teach our girls to inflict violence upon one another—on the contrary, our aim is to produce fine, upstanding young ladies who are well aware of their place in society and who will, it is hoped, be a credit to their school and their country. Any girl found fighting is swiftly dealt with, and Barbara can be no exception.'

'Oh!' said Angela, surprised. 'Are you quite certain? That's not like her at all. Did you ask her why she had done it?'

'Yes, but she refused absolutely to answer,' said Miss Bell. 'She was quite intransigent in the matter, and therefore I had no choice but to tell her that, given her shocking behaviour, I should be unable to keep her at the school any longer.'

Angela's heart sank. What on earth had possessed the girl?

Miss Bell went across to the window and stood, gazing out at the fruits of her labour as they gambolled happily on the lawn.

'It is a great pity,' she said. 'Barbara is a very able child in most subjects, but especially Mathematics—as you have just seen. If she would only apply herself to use her talents in a more useful direction, then I should have no doubt of her achieving great success in life. I am particularly disappointed to have to let her go, since I had been planning to put her forward for extra tuition in Maths and Geometry. You know, of course, that the school was founded with the express purpose of preparing girls to sit the Cambridge entrance examination, and I had every hope that Barbara would pass it with no difficulty at all. Mathematics was my own favourite subject at school, and I take a particular interest in girls who show an aptitude for it. Unfortunately, we have another girl with a gift for the discipline who looks almost certain to leave Wakeley Court soon, as she is from one of the less wealthy families and they are having difficulty with the fees. Of course, the school is an expensive one, but we do our utmost to offer assistance to talented girls whose families would otherwise be unable to afford to send them here. As it happens, Violet Smedley is already the possessor of two scholarships, but it appears that even they will not be sufficient to enable her to stay at Wakeley Court, and there are no other scholarships available. It pains me to lose two such pupils at once.' Here she gave a deep sigh.

Angela had been only half-listening, for she was absorbed in thoughts of having to send off for prospectuses, write letters explaining why Barbara needed to change school halfway through the term, wait anxiously for replies and then perhaps find that no-one was prepared to accept the girl at all. And what would she do then? She looked up to find the headmistress gazing at her speculatively.

'I beg your pardon, what did you say?' she said. 'Something about scholarships?'

'I was speaking of Violet Smedley,' said Miss Bell. 'She is a poor girl whom I believe to be capable of great things if given the opportunity.'

She paused and coughed significantly.

Angela had the notion that something was wanted of her, but could not tell what.

'And you say she will have to leave the school as her parents cannot afford the fees?' she said.

'I am afraid so,' said Miss Bell, eyeing Angela's expensively-tailored dress and jacket.

Suddenly Angela understood, although for a second she could hardly believe it. She looked at Miss Bell in surprise, saw the way out which was being offered her, and made an upwards adjustment in her estimation of the headmistress's abilities. It would be expensive, but the case was an urgent one and Angela saw that she had no choice but to rise to the occasion. She hesitated, then cleared her throat.

'This Violet Smedley—is she a well-behaved girl?' she said.

'She is an absolute credit to the school,' said Miss Bell. 'Her conduct in all respects is exemplary.'

'It is a pity I'd never heard of her before,' said Angela, feeling her way carefully. 'Had I known about her I should have encouraged Barbara to become friends with her, in the hope that Barbara might be induced to follow her example.'

Here she glanced up and thought she saw the merest glimmer of approval in Miss Bell's eye, but the other woman said nothing, merely waited.

'Do you imagine Barbara to be beyond all possibility of improvement?' Angela went on.

'Not at all,' said Miss Bell. 'On the contrary, I believe her to be a very good girl at heart, but one who tends to

choose the wrong company. If she were to form a friend-
ship with a quiet, steady girl, for example, I have no doubt
that she would settle down considerably.'

'Such as Violet, you mean? Yes, I think you are most
likely right. It is a great pity, then, that you have been
forced to expel Barbara before she could make a friend of
that sort,' said Angela, glancing at Miss Bell sideways. 'As
you say, setting aside the naughtiness, she's clever enough.
I'm sure you would have liked to see her and this Violet
pass the entrance examination with flying colours, if only
for the benefit of the school and its reputation.'

'I certainly should,' said Miss Bell. She regarded
Angela encouragingly, as she might a girl who had made it
halfway through her task without mistakes.

'I was rather keen on Mathematics myself when I was
younger,' Angela went on, more confident now of what
was required, 'and I always rather thought that I should
like to endow a scholarship one day, if the opportunity
presented itself. However, it never did. It's unfortunate that
my connection with the school is about to end, since it
sounds as though Violet Smedley would have been a most
deserving recipient of such a scholarship.'

'Indeed she would,' said Miss Bell, 'and I shall go so far
as to say that I think Violet herself would have benefited
enormously from having a companion such as Barbara
with whom to work towards the examination.'

'Then it is a shame that both of them will be leaving
the school shortly,' said Angela.

'Yes, it is, isn't it?' said Miss Bell.

There followed a pause loaded with meaning. The two
ladies' eyes met.

Chapter Three

BARBARA WAS STANDING outside Miss Bell's study, under the watchful eye of the headmistress's secretary, when Angela emerged. Angela regarded the girl. She had the scraggy, lanky aspect of a child who had grown a lot in the past year, and her hair looked as though she had not combed it in a week. She gave Angela a wary but slightly defiant glance.

'Well?' she said.

'I should like a word with you, Barbara,' said Angela. 'Let us go into the grounds.'

This was hardly a surprise, so Barbara set her jaw, followed Angela into the corridor, and prepared for a roasting. She thanked her stars that the Ellises were abroad, since the thought of an hour or two on the carpet at home, staring mutinously at the floor while Gerald strode up and down and tore at his hair and Nina gave full vent to her sharp tongue, did not appeal. The mild-mannered Angela was a much better prospect, thought Barbara, and felt somewhat cheered.

They headed out through the Quad and away from the

building, and stopped by the tennis courts, which were quite deserted for once. Angela regarded Barbara coolly for a good long minute, until the girl felt quite awkward under her gaze and began to wonder whether she had drawn the easy lot after all.

'Must you be so silent?' she said nervously at last. 'Can't you just get it over with?'

'I should like to hear what you have to say for yourself first,' said Angela.

Barbara looked sulky.

'What's the use?' she said. 'I suppose you've heard it all from Big Ben, and I can't deny any of it, so why must we go over it again? She's given me the chuck now, anyhow, and I don't suppose there's any chance of her changing her mind, so why don't we just can it and shove off?'

'Is that the sort of language they teach you here?' said Angela. 'If so, perhaps it's a good thing you're leaving.'

'No,' admitted Barbara. 'They're rather hot on our not using slang. I'd get a fine and a black mark for it.'

'Then you'll think before you speak and not add to your list of misdeeds if you know what's good for you,' said Angela. 'I have just spent a most uncomfortable hour in the company of your headmistress, hearing all sorts of tales about what you have been getting up to, and I am not in the best of moods at present. Now, kindly explain yourself. What do you think Nina and Gerald are going to say when they find out you have been expelled in disgrace? Is this any way to repay their kind treatment of you?'

Her tone was icy and Barbara reddened.

'I'm sorry, Angela. It was only supposed to be a bit of fun. I try to be good, truly I do, but then the devil gets into me and I can't help getting into scrapes.'

'What do you mean, you can't help it?' said Angela. 'You are fourteen, not four. One would expect that by now you would have at least some semblance of control over your baser impulses. Can't you even get through one term without playing some silly trick or other?'

'That's pretty thick,' said Barbara indignantly. 'The book was your idea. You told me yourself you did something similar when you were at school.'

Angela blinked as the conversation in question came back to her, but barely faltered.

'Firstly, it was not "my idea," as you put it,' she said. 'At no point did I instruct you to do the same thing. As a matter of fact, I believe I expressly mentioned it as an example of my naughtiness as a child and told you *not* to do it. Secondly, I played the trick on the prefects, not the mistresses, which is a different thing entirely and not nearly so disrespectful. And thirdly,' she could not help adding, 'when *I* did it, I was never stupid enough to get caught.' She was aware that this fact hardly constituted the moral high ground, and so went on hurriedly, 'How did Miss Bell get hold of the book?'

'I don't know,' said Barbara. 'I think someone must have snitched. Probably the Everard female. It would be like her.'

'Who is the Everard female?' said Angela.

'Edith Everard,' said Barbara. 'Horrid thing. She hates me but I'm not scared of her. She knows it and that's probably why she tried to get me into trouble. Awful bully. She gives the smaller girls a terrible time of it and I won't stand for it.'

'Is she the girl you shoved?' said Angela.

'Yes,' said Barbara defiantly, 'and I shouldn't have stopped there if Miss Devlin hadn't caught me.'

'But why?' said Angela. 'That's not like you at all, Barbara.'

'I hate bullying,' said Barbara, 'and I won't stand for it.'

'Who was she bullying?' said Angela.

'Oh, just one of the scholarship girls,' said Barbara. 'It's hardly their fault if their people don't have much money, is it? And looking down on them for being poor is a low thing to do. Edith's uncle is a baronet, or something, although I heard he was disgraced, and she seems to think that gives her the right to lord it over everybody. It's not as though a baronet is all that impressive anyway. We have all sorts of high-born girls here—why, we've even got a foreign princess, but *she* doesn't give herself any airs. She's rather dull, as a matter of fact.'

'But Barbara,' said Angela, 'why didn't you tell Miss Bell all this at the time?'

'Because girls don't squeak on one another,' said Barbara. 'It simply isn't done.'

'But you just said this Everard girl squeaked on you.'

'Yes, and that just goes to show what a vile pig she is, don't you see?' said Barbara.

'Barbara!' exclaimed Angela.

'Sorry,' muttered Barbara.

Angela looked at the girl's hot, mutinous face, and felt a pang of sympathy mixed in with the exasperation, for she had been just the same at Barbara's age—although without quite so many opportunities for mischief. It was perfectly evident that Barbara had reached a delicate stage in which she would need careful handling; otherwise, she looked likely to run off the rails altogether and become quite incorrigible. Summoning the Ellises back from their trip was wholly out of the question, however—and indeed, Angela harboured no small feelings of guilt at having left so much of Barbara's care to them over the years. They had been only too willing to provide her with a happy, healthy family life that would otherwise have been lacking, but it was not fair that they should be forced to take *all* the

responsibility upon themselves. Angela saw that the time
had come for her to begin taking greater pains with the girl
now that she was growing up, and relieve Nina and Gerald
of some of the burden. As one of Barbara's guardians it
was only right that she should do so. Having reached this
decision (with the additional faint hope that it might
assuage some of her uncomfortable feelings on the question), Angela abandoned all thoughts of the trip to Paris—
not without reluctance—and resolved that from now on
she should keep a closer eye on Barbara's progress. Perhaps
a little kind treatment now would do her good—although
there was still the matter of the threatened expulsion from
Wakeley Court to be got over, and on that there was still
much to be said. Angela drew herself up, hardened her
heart and prepared to deliver a lecture.

'Listen to me,' she said. 'I don't know why on earth you
thought you could get away with this sort of behaviour
without being punished. It's all very well saying you can't
help it, but I'm afraid that's no good. You simply *must* help
it. Think how tremendously selfish you're being by acting
like this.'

'Selfish?' said Barbara, taken aback, for truth to tell she
rather considered herself to be a sort of female Robin
Hood, entertaining and protecting her fellow pupils at no
little cost to herself.

'Yes, selfish,' said Angela with emphasis. 'Just think
what would have happened had I not been here to fetch
you. Nina and Gerald would have had to come all the way
back from India just to get you out of this scrape. It was
the only opportunity they had to see Richard and to meet
Emma and the new baby, and you might have spoilt it all
for them—not least because you know perfectly well they
wouldn't have hesitated. I must say, I'm very disappointed
in you, Barbara. The Ellises have treated you like a daugh-

ter. You've wanted for nothing, and this is how you repay them: by getting yourself expelled from school—and that's after you've already been moved once at your own request. You ought at least to have made a little effort. I don't know where you learned such ingratitude, but I think you might have the grace to be ashamed of yourself for it.'

Barbara shuffled uncomfortably.

'I say, Angela,' she said. 'There's no need to make one feel quite such a worm.'

'Oh, but there is,' said Angela. 'You are now of an age in which you ought to be aware of the possible consequences of your actions. By losing your place at this school you have most likely forfeited any chance you had of passing the Cambridge entrance examination, and that is something from which you will suffer for the rest of your life. How do you expect to make anything of yourself without a good education? You might find it funny to throw eggs at people now, but I can assure you it won't look so funny in a few years when you discover that you've wasted all your opportunities because of it—always assuming, of course, that you're not planning a career as a circus clown.'

'All right, then, I'm sorry,' said Barbara grumpily. 'I'm sorry I've been such a burden to everyone. But it doesn't matter, does it? It's not as though I really need an education. I mean to say, I can just wait until I'm twenty-one and come into my money, and then I can go off around the world and have adventures, and you'll all be rid of me.'

'It's not a question of being rid of you,' said Angela. 'And besides, there's no certainty that you *will* get your money then. That all depends on the trustees—and since I am one of them I may as well tell you now that you won't get a penny of it unless I see some sign of improvement in you very soon indeed.'

'Oh!' said Barbara, who had rather relished the idea of travelling the world, dispensing largesse to the deserving. 'I didn't know you were a trustee.'

'Yes,' said Angela. 'And I won't agree to your having the money until I'm certain you can be relied upon not to do something stupid with it. I should hate you to be an idiot and end up falling prey to a fortune-hunter, as—' Here she broke off, for she had almost said, 'as I did.' She coughed, and went on, '—as soon as you get your hands on it.'

'But I shouldn't,' said Barbara. 'I'm far too sensible for that.'

'Not on current showing,' said Angela.

They stood in silence then, since Barbara looked as though she were thinking and Angela judged it better to let her reflect on her sins for a few minutes. They gazed in the direction of the lake, from where the sound of laughter floated towards them. Two girls appeared to have taken a third girl's shoe, and were tossing it about between them while the other chased them and tried to get it back. Eventually they all fell down in a flurry of arms and legs and the laughter became louder.

'I shall be sorry to leave, I suppose,' said Barbara at last. 'It's not a bad place, really.'

Angela said nothing.

'And I *was* doing rather well in Maths,' went on Barbara. 'I was doing lessons with the Fifth, you know, and Big Ben—Miss Bell, I mean—said something about putting me in with them for some other subjects too if I carried on as I had been doing.'

She looked a little wistful.

'Miss Bell praised your Mathematics abilities very highly,' said Angela, who felt that some encouragement was needed.

'I'm not the best in the year,' said Barbara. 'Violet Smedley is cleverer than I am, but she doesn't get everything right. I'm better at algebra. We compete against each other. Or we did, anyway,' she finished sadly. 'She's leaving too.'

'Is she a friend of yours?' said Angela.

'She's all right,' said Barbara. 'Quiet. A little dull, I should think.'

There was a long pause, then:

'I'm sorry, Angela,' Barbara said quietly. 'I've let you all down, haven't I?'

'Yes,' said Angela. 'You have, rather.'

'I wish there were something I could do to put it right. I knew I'd get into trouble if anybody caught me with that book, but the other girls egged me on, and—'

She stopped as she saw Angela's expression.

'I suppose I oughtn't to put the blame on others for what I did,' she said.

'No,' agreed Angela. 'Nobody forced you, I imagine.'

'No, of course they didn't. It was all my idea. I dare say I'm just naturally bad.'

'You're not bad at all,' said Angela. 'But you are very thoughtless at times.'

'Yes, I am,' said Barbara. 'I shall try harder in future, Angela, I promise. But what am I to do now? I've been given the chuck. Where am I to go? Nina and Gerald are away, and I know you're always too busy to look after me. Do you suppose they'll let me stay here until another school can be found?'

'As a matter of fact, you've been given a reprieve,' said Angela, suppressing a pang at the 'too busy' remark.

Barbara glanced up in surprise.

'What?' she said, staring. 'Do you mean to say Miss

Bell has changed her mind? Then I'm not to be expelled after all?'

'It appears not,' said Angela. She went on quickly as she saw the dawning delight on Barbara's face, 'There are, of course, conditions attached.'

'Yes, yes,' said Barbara eagerly. 'They'll want me to be good, I know that. I shall be a perfect angel, I promise. I'll learn all my lessons on time, and I'll stop cheeking the mistresses, especially Miss Devlin—although it's *so* hard to resist, sometimes—and I'll stop all the silly betting, and —and—'

'And you'll apologize to Edith Everard,' said Angela.

'What?' cried Barbara in dismay. 'But—'

'But nothing,' said Angela. 'Miss Bell was quite firm on the subject, and so am I. You will make a formal apology to Edith Everard for shoving her in the corridor.'

'But it's so unfair,' said Barbara. 'She's the one who caused the trouble.'

'Nonetheless, if you wish to continue at the school, then that is what you will do,' said Angela. 'You will tell her you are sorry and give every appearance of meaning it, whether you do or not. You may continue to think of her as you choose, naturally.'

Barbara saw that she had no option.

'Very well,' she said. 'I'll do it.'

'Good,' said Angela. 'Now, then, we had better go and speak to Miss Bell. I imagine she is preparing a number of other punishments for you in the matter of lines, detentions, and so forth, but I dare say you've had plenty of experience of those.'

'Oh yes, I get them all the time. I don't know why they bother, to be honest, since it doesn't do a thing to stop me,' said Barbara with disarming frankness.

'So I see,' said Angela.

They set off briskly back towards the Quad. Barbara was very nearly as tall as Angela now, and had no difficulty in keeping up.

'I say,' she said suddenly, as a thought struck her. 'Did *you* persuade her to keep me on, Angela? What did you say to her?'

'I—er—merely pointed out all your many good qualities, and promised her that you would behave impeccably in future, and so she agreed to give you another chance,' said Angela. 'Not that you deserve it,' she added.

She had gained no little respect for Miss Bell during their interview. The headmistress had proved herself to be unexpectedly sharp and less wedded to convention than might have been supposed from her appearance, given that she had shown no compunction in soliciting what amounted to a bribe in return for keeping Barbara. Their talk had ended with a shake of hands, warm thanks from Miss Bell, and an invitation to visit the school properly as an honoured guest in a week or two. Of course, there would be formalities to complete with regard to the endowment of the scholarship, but the headmistress had waved all that away as a matter of no moment for the present. It was so encouraging, she said with a perfectly straight face, to find that there were still so many benefactors—and benefactresses—who were prepared to support the education of girls with such generosity. It was doubly important that this should be so now that the universities were starting to admit women. Meanwhile, Angela nodded and smiled and thought to herself that this Violet Smedley had better be all she was cracked up to be, since she had just cost Angela rather a lot of money.

As they entered the building, they encountered a bland young man in mortar-board and gown who was carrying a sheaf of papers.

'Hallo, sir,' said Barbara cheerfully.

'Ah—hallo—er—Barbara,' said the man, glancing up. 'I hope you have learned your task for today's lesson.'

'I think so,' said Barbara. '*Sic fatur lacrimans*, wasn't it? By the way, this is Mrs. Marchmont. You've probably heard of her. Angela, this is our new Latin master, Mr. Hesketh.'

'It is a pleasure to meet you, Mrs. Marchmont,' said Mr. Hesketh, and shook Angela's hand. Angela thought she saw a look of curiosity pass across his face, but it swiftly disappeared and was replaced by an expression of nothing more than polite interest. 'Have you come to look around the school?'

'No,' said the irrepressible Barbara. 'She came to save me from being expelled. She's a darling.'

'Ah,' said Mr. Hesketh. 'Jolly good.' There was little else that could be said on the subject without awkwardness, and so he smiled politely and passed on.

'There's no need to tell everyone,' said Angela. 'It's not something to be proud of, you know.'

'Sorry, Angela,' said Barbara.

It was clear that her subdued mood was already beginning to wear off, and so Angela hurried her along to the headmistress's study to act the penitent as required before Miss Bell could change her mind.

Chapter Four

A FEW DAYS after her return to London, Angela received with her morning post a letter that puzzled her very much. She sat and frowned over it in silence until her maid, Marthe, could not help asking about it.

'It is not bad news, I hope, *madame*,' she said.

'No,' said Angela, still frowning. 'At least, I don't think so. It's from Henry Jameson. He would like to see me at my earliest convenience. Now, what on earth can he possibly want? The letter is typewritten and signed by a secretary so it can't be personal business. How odd.'

'Shall you go?' said Marthe.

'Of course I shall,' said Angela. 'It doesn't do to say no to British Intelligence. And besides, I'm awfully curious to find out what it's all about.'

Accordingly, that afternoon, Angela presented herself at the entrance of a grey and unassuming building located on a certain side-street off Whitehall, and asked to see Mr. Jameson. She was immediately taken up to the third floor and shown into the presence of the man himself. Henry Jameson was as unassuming as his office, and looked far too comfortable to be the head of Intelligence. He rose to greet her as she entered, and twinkled at her through his round spectacles.

'Hallo, Angela,' he said. 'I see you got my letter.'

'Hallo, Henry. I certainly did,' she replied, 'and I'm simply dying to know what it's all about. I assume you didn't call me here to discuss your brother's forthcoming wedding.'

He laughed.

'No, of course not,' he said. 'Although I understand you were largely responsible for it.'

'It was nothing to do with me,' said Angela. 'I just happened to be there at the time. I'm tremendously pleased, of course.'

'So are we all,' he assured her. 'It will do him good to have something to think about other than his job for a change. All work and no play, and all that, what?'

'Oh, yes,' said Angela. 'So, then,' she said, once they were seated, 'why did you wish to see me? Is it to do with the business at Fives Castle last winter?'

'No, no,' he said. 'That was all resolved quite satisfacto-rily—from our point of view, at least.'

'Then what is it?'

He regarded her for a moment, then said:

'Of course, you understand that anything we say here must not go beyond these four walls.'

'Naturally,' said Angela.

'Very good,' he said. He hesitated, then to Angela's surprise, went on, 'I understand you have a niece at Wakeley Court school.'

Whatever Angela had expected, it was not that.

'Not a niece, but a god-daughter,' she said in momentary fear of what Barbara might have been getting up to now. 'But yes, Barbara is a pupil at Wakeley Court.'

'Oh? I beg your pardon. My informant was under the impression that the two of you were related. Still, it doesn't matter. She is not the person with whom we are concerned.'

'I'm glad to hear it,' said Angela, relieved. 'I take it you have a particular interest in the school, then.'

Henry nodded.

'We do at present, at any rate,' he said.

'Is the place crawling with foreign spies?' inquired Angela, not entirely seriously.

'Not as far as we are aware,' said Henry, 'although if you spot any I should be obliged if you would let me know. No, our interest in the school is due to the presence there of a pupil of some importance. Have you heard of Morania?'

'Yes, of course,' said Angela. 'It's a small country somewhere near Bulgaria or Rumania, if I remember correctly.'

'That's right,' said Henry. 'It's one of those places that seem to have been stuck in the dark ages for centuries. You know the sort of country I mean: mostly agricultural with little mechanized industry, still ruled by a monarch—a Grand Duke, I should say—rather than an elected govern-ment. All very ceremonial, and of little interest to the rest of the world.'

He paused.

'"Until now," you're going to say,' said Angela with a smile.

'Exactly,' said Henry. 'Until now. I said that Morania was mediaeval, but as a matter of fact that's not quite true. Much to everybody's surprise, their current Grand Duke has proved to be something of a reformer. Since the war he has built railways and factories, introduced new and more efficient ways of doing things, and made every attempt to improve the lot of the poorest people in the land—partly by giving them the vote.'

'Oh, yes, I think I read something about that,' said Angela. 'I gather the aristocracy weren't too happy about it.'

'No,' said Henry. 'There wasn't much they could do about it, though, since Grand Duke Feodor seems to be a pretty determined chap and is rather good at playing his enemies off against one another in order to get what he wants.'

'Clever of him.'

'Indeed it is. Now, as you may know, Morania has spent the past five hundred years or so in a state of more or less permanent hostility with its neighbour, Krovodar. Krovodar is another small nation, but it is in a much worse state than Morania. For the past fifty years it has suffered from corrupt and unstable governments, who have spent most of their time fighting with each other in an attempt to appropriate the country's rich natural resources for them-selves. As a result, most Krovodanians live in poverty and the place as a whole is pretty miserable.'

'Didn't Morania and Krovodar agree some sort of truce a few years ago?' said Angela.

'Yes, they did. The two countries are officially on good terms these days, although the peace is slightly strained—only to be expected considering that they've been at each other's throats practically since the dawn of time. The *détente* has been largely the work of Grand Duke Feodor, who believes that a closer alliance is the best way to advance and enrich both countries. As I said, Krovodar is blessed with an abundance of natural resources, but has not exploited them for the good of its people. The Grand Duke has put a great deal of effort into securing mining and trading agreements between

Morania and Krovodar, with the intent of forging a closer alliance between the two countries and improving the lot of everyone.'

'This Grand Duke sounds like a splendid fellow,' observed Angela.

'Oh, he is,' agreed Henry. 'And of course, as is the way of things, that means that half the world are out for his blood.'

'Dear me,' said Angela. 'How unfortunate. Anybody in particular?'

'We're not quite sure, yet,' said Henry, 'but there are plenty of vultures circling. As I said, in the past we haven't generally concerned ourselves with what the minnows get up to, but of course the balance of power has changed completely since the war—and especially since the Russians decided they had no further use for their royal family and disposed of them like so much rubbish.'

'Ah,' said Angela. 'Do you consider the Grand Duke to be a stabilizing influence on that part of the world?'

'We do,' said Henry. 'And it's in our interest to keep him alive as long as possible. We don't want the Russians getting any ideas. They're greedy enough for territory as it is.'

'What makes you think the Grand Duke is in particular danger now?'

'Only what he, or rather his second minister, told us,' said Henry. 'Given their lively history, the Moranians tend to keep a watchful eye out for any likely attempts on their royal family. The Ivanovetis have ruled the country for six hundred years or more, and one doesn't hold on to power in a country such as Morania without having a pretty efficient intelligence system in place. I understand from this minister, Count Paul, who is apparently a sort of commoner cousin of the Grand Duke, that they have received word of an assassination plot cooked up by Krovodar itself.'

'Oh dear,' said Angela. 'But why should they want to kill him if he's been doing his best to help them? It seems a rather low thing to do.'

'It's perfectly understandable if you look at it from Krovodar's point of view, though. They have a weak government and a restless populace who might revolt at any moment, so what better way to distract everybody's attention than by causing trouble elsewhere? It's a logical enough step to take. There is a region of Morania called Iszbicka, which is on the border with Krovodar and which was once part of that country. It has a large Krovodanian population, and for centuries there have been rumblings about returning the region to Krovodar, although nothing has ever come of it. Fomenting border trouble would be the perfect distraction from problems at home.'

'Of course,' said Angela.

'According to the intelligence we have,' Henry went on, 'the plan is to assassinate the Grand Duke and then annex Iszbicka in all the confusion. You see, the Grand Duke's greatest weakness lies in the fact that his line has almost died out. The last of the Ivanovetis is a fifteen-year-old girl, who will inherit the throne in default of any suitable male heirs, since the only other possible candidates are second and third cousins of the family who were exiled many years ago after being caught plotting against the present Grand Duke's father. From the Ivanovetis' point of view, it is of the utmost importance that Princess Irina make a suitable marriage as soon as she is old enough, and produce an heir—or preferably several. That will not take place for some years yet, however, and in the meantime, if the Grand Duke were to be assassinated then a vacuum would be created that might lead to all sorts of unpleasantness.'

'I see,' said Angela. 'You think that while Krovodar was busy invading Iszbicka, the Russians would take the opportunity to invade the rest of Morania?'

'Morania, Iszbicka, and probably Krovodar itself,' said Henry. 'And who knows whether they'd stop there? I shouldn't be surprised if they decided that since they'd gone to the trouble of leaving the house, they might as well grab a couple of other countries too while they were out.'

Angela could not help laughing at his undiplomatic turn of phrase.

'It does seem rather worrying,' she said. 'But what has it all to do with Wakeley Court?'

'I was just coming to that,' said Henry. 'The fact is that Princess Irina has started as a pupil there this year.'

'Oh? She has been sent there for safety, I assume.'

'I gather they had been planning to send her to school anyway,' said Henry, 'but when this all came out it gave them an added motive to get her out of the country, since there is some hint that the Krovodanians want to assassinate her too. She was brought up in England until she was about ten years old, I believe, and her father is keen for her to continue her English education.'

'Barbara said something about a foreign princess at Wakeley Court,' said Angela, remembering. 'But can the school protect this girl from her enemies? It hardly seems the sort of place that would be equipped for that kind of thing.'

'Nobody in Morania knows she is here,' said Henry. 'The plan was carried out in secret.'

'But then why is her name known at the school?'

Henry sighed.

'These things soon get out,' he said. 'As I said, they had been expecting her at Wakeley Court before this story of the assassination attempt came out, so the news was already known to many when she arrived, even though they tried not to make too much of it. She is enrolled at the school under the name Irina Ivanoveti, and although I imagine not everybody is aware of who she is, many certainly are.'

'That is rather unfortunate,' said Angela.

'It is not as bad as it seems,' said Henry. 'As you know, the school is in a fairly remote part of Norfolk, close to the North coast, and anybody unfamiliar arriving in the area would be spotted immediately. Besides, as soon as we knew of the danger I sent a man to the school to keep an eye on things. It was he who informed me that you had been visiting the place.'

'Mr. Hesketh,' said Angela in sudden understanding.

'Yes, that's the chap. Reggie Hesketh. You spotted him, did you?'

'No, not at all. I had no idea until now.'

'Good. We don't want everyone knowing who he is. He is posing as a Latin master—as a matter of fact he is very well qualified to teach several languages, and he is one of our most capable men.'

'It sounds like you have everything in hand,' said Angela. 'But what do you want with me?'

Henry looked uncomfortable.

'I don't like it, Angela,' he said. 'Looking at it objectively, the whole thing might be a mare's nest, since we've received no intelligence ourselves of anything bubbling under the surface in that part of the world, and to tell the truth the Moranians do tend to be a bit over-sensitive about what they perceive as threats to their safety, so we generally don't pay too much attention. Still, I've been in this job a long time and learnt to trust my instincts, and I've a feeling in my bones that something's not right, although I couldn't tell you what. I feel as though I haven't been told the whole story—that something is missing.'

'But what am I to do? You already have a man in place.'

'True, but there is a limit to what he can do. If something is going on then we need to know what is happening at the school—not just among the teachers, you understand, but also among the pupils—and of course, Hesketh is not allowed to get too pally with the girls. The school is extremely strict about that sort of thing, and Miss Bell, the headmistress, watches the male teachers like a hawk. They're not even allowed in the main building after seven o'clock. If Hesketh were a woman it would be a different matter, but we don't have any women in the department who are suitably qualified. It was just pure good luck that the school happened to be looking for a Latin master and that Hesketh is so hot on languages—otherwise we'd have had to send someone to watch from the outside, which wouldn't have been the same thing at all.'

'No,' agreed Angela.

'I think something is going on there,' continued Henry, 'and I want to know what it is. I don't suppose you noticed anything odd yourself when you were there?'

'Such as what?' said Angela. 'Do you mean mysterious foreigners brandishing carved daggers in a menacing fashion, that sort of thing?'

'It does sound rather far-fetched when you put it like that,' said Henry.

'I'm sorry,' said Angela. 'Facetious of me. No, I'm afraid I didn't notice anything. I was there on a matter connected with Barbara, and so that was uppermost in my mind at the time. I wasn't really paying much attention to anything else. However, I have been invited by Miss Bell to return to Wakeley Court next week, and I can keep an eye out then, if you like, although I don't suppose I will notice anything that Mr. Hesketh has missed.'

'Would you?' said Henry. 'That would be splendid. As you say, you probably won't find anything out, but you may get an opportunity to speak to the girls and see if any of them have noticed anything. You'll have to be careful about it, though. We need to keep the thing absolutely secret.'

Angela promised to do her best, and thus the matter was agreed.

Chapter Five

THE WARM WEATHER continued at Wakeley Court, which inclined the girls to be sluggish and made the teachers' efforts to introduce a little knowledge into their pupils' heads somewhat more difficult than was generally the case at that time of year. The girls took every opportunity they could to spend time out of doors, and on any given lunch-time the lawns could be seen dotted with blue and brown tunics, and fluttering white exercise-books, as everyone took their work outside and did it there—or at least, pretended to.

On one such lunch-time Barbara Wells could be found sitting on the grass close to the edge of the lake, with several of the members of her 'set'. Following her near escape from being expelled ten days earlier, Barbara had been taking some pains to improve her behaviour, and had been so successful in her efforts that the only thing on which she might have been pulled up that day was the theft of a bag of apples, which she had abstracted neatly when the kitchen-maids' backs were turned. The little group were now disposing of the evidence with great efficiency, while Barbara absently read over her History essay, which she had just received back that morning covered with rather more red ink than was admirable.

No snob herself, Barbara had taken to heart the insistence by Miss Bell and Angela that she make friends with the scholarship girl Violet Smedley. Whether or not the quiet, obedient Violet had been informed of the circumstances under which she had been allowed to stay at Wakeley Court was not clear; nonetheless, she had accepted Barbara's overtures with patient resignation at first, and after a few days of being subjected to a barrage of enthusiastic friendliness had even begun to find Barbara and her noisy friends rather likable. Barbara had not stopped there, however. When she turned over a new leaf she liked to do it thoroughly, and she had kindly taken it upon herself to bring two other girls within her sphere of influence while she was about it. One of these was Irina Ivanoveti, on whom Barbara had taken pity as many of the girls knew she was a princess and seemed in awe of the fact, as a result of which she was frequently left alone. When Irina was not present the other members of the group secretly agreed that she wasn't much fun, since she had a half-fearful, half-sulky manner that hardly recommended her to them—but Barbara had insisted and so they accepted her as good-naturedly as they could.

Barbara now looked up from her essay and prodded Irina with her toe.

'I say, Irina,' she said. 'You're the first member of royalty I've met. Do you wear a crown when you're not at school?'

'Idiot,' said Isabel Chambers, who was almost Barbara's equal for mischief as a general rule. 'Of course she doesn't.'

'Well, then, what about your father?' said Barbara. 'He's the King, isn't he?'

'He's a Grand Duke, not a King,' put in Florrie Evans, before Irina had a chance to reply. 'He still rules the country, though, isn't that right?'

'Yes,' said Irina hesitantly, with a glance at Florrie.

'But does he wear a crown?' persisted Barbara. 'Isn't it a bit heavy? I should have thought it would leave a nasty red mark around his head after a few hours.'

Irina looked taken aback and Florrie giggled.

'You've shocked her,' she said. 'I'll bet nobody has ever dared ask her that before.'

Florrie was the other new girl to whom Barbara had taken a fancy. She was a dark-haired girl whose usually serious expression belied a lively sense of humour. She was in the Fifth with Irina, but since Barbara did some of her lessons with that form there was no barrier to their becoming firm friends.

'Crowns are worn only on ceremonial occasions,' said Irina at last in her careful, halting English. 'My father prefers to dress in the manner of an ordinary man most of the time. During the formal occasions he wears velvet robes trimmed with ermine and mink, but that is not very often.'

'Does he gallop through the streets of the city on a white horse, swiping at peasants with his sword as he passes?' inquired Barbara.

Florrie giggled again.

'Please?' said Irina in astonishment. She looked around at the amused faces of the group, and her brow cleared.

'Oh, I understand—you are teasing me,' she said.

'Only a little bit,' said Barbara. 'That's what we do in England. We like to make fun of each other. You may laugh at *me* now if you like,' she said generously. 'Look what Miss Finch has written on my essay.'

Florrie grabbed the exercise-book before Irina could move and examined the comment in Miss Finch's neat handwriting underneath Barbara's *opus*.

'"Perhaps if you were to listen more carefully during lessons, you would be aware that Eleanor of Aquitaine was married to the *second* King Henry, not the *eighth*,"' she read, '"although this misapprehension may go some way towards explaining your apparent belief that Thomas à Becket and Thomas More were one and the same person."'

Barbara accepted her rallying with good humour.

'Miss Finch is a stiff one,' said Isabel. 'Does anyone ever get a good mark from her?'

'I do, sometimes,' said Violet, and had an exercise-book thrown at her head for her trouble.

'I've got a question for you,' said Barbara, after a pause. 'If you were stranded in the jungle and certain to die without help, which of the teachers should you prefer to have with you?'

'Miss Devlin,' said Melisande Bartlett-Hendry, another member of the group. 'She's the strongest and could build a shelter. Did you see her lifting that vaulting-horse all by herself the other day? I'm pretty certain that if we met any cannibals she could fight them all off with her bare hands.'

'As a matter of fact, I think Miss Finch would be good in a tight spot,' said Violet. 'Yes, she's sharp-tongued, but there's no nonsense about her. She'd know what to do.'

'Definitely *not* Miss Fazackerley,' said Isabel.

'Ugh, no,' agreed Barbara. 'I'm glad I don't have her for Maths any more. She's such a lump.'

Everyone agreed that Miss Fazackerley was indeed a lump.

Just then, Mr. Welland, the English master—he of the

Byronic locks and soulful eyes—walked past, ignoring everyone as he went by. Several of the girls sighed.

'Dear, sweet Augustus, how distant you are,' said Melisande sentimentally in the direction of the departing master's back. 'Do you know, I dropped my handkerchief in the passage the other day, and he *picked it up* for me. I shall treasure it forever.'

'You cat!' said Rosabelle Masefield, the last member of the group. 'I'm horribly jealous. When he read out *The Lady of Shalott* the other day I couldn't help but picture him as Sir Lancelot, riding through the school in his armour. He has such a courtly look about him.'

'Pfft!' said Barbara. 'I happen to know he lives with his mother in the village, in that flat above the post-office. I'll bet she makes him wear a flannel vest even in summer.'

This last supposition was roundly rejected as impossible for a man of such noble appearance.

'Miss Bell hardly lets him even talk to us,' complained Rosabelle.

'I don't know why,' said Barbara. 'He never shows the slightest bit of interest in the girls. You two would be better off sighing for old Penkridge, even if he is about ninety-eight.'

The girls all giggled. Mr. Welland strolled on, and whether or not his broad, clear brow in sunlight glow'd, it was certainly untroubled by any awareness of the attention it had excited.

'What about Mam'selle, then?' said Isabel, returning to the original question.

They all thought about it.

'I love Mam'selle,' said Barbara, 'but she'd be no use in the jungle. Not for our purposes, at any rate. She's far too smart to do any of the hard work herself. She'd find a way of getting us to do it while she sat there, smiling approvingly and making encouraging noises.'

At that moment, Lydia Chambers, the head girl, turned up.

'Where did you get those apples?' she said. 'Barbara, have you been taking food from the kitchen again?'

'Can't you let it go this once?' said Isabel, who was Lydia's younger sister and took as much advantage as possible of the fact. 'That stew we had for lunch was simply vile. It must be Cook's day off.'

'Either that or the butcher's was closed and they had to round up some stray dogs to put in it,' said Barbara. 'I'm sure I found a nose in mine.'

There were howls of disgust followed by giggling.

'That's enough,' said Lydia sharply. 'Any more of that and I'll have to report you to Miss Finch.'

'Sorry, Lydia,' said Barbara, not sounding sorry at all. 'Have an apple?'

Lydia hesitated and glanced about her.

'Oh, well,' she said. 'They do look rather nice, and the stew *was* pretty awful. Don't tell anyone, though.' She took an apple and passed on.

Barbara stretched herself out on the grass.

'I wish something exciting would happen,' she said. 'Things have been awfully dull lately. If I hadn't promised to be good we might go up on the roof. But I suppose it's better not to risk it.'

'I don't like it up there anyway,' said Melisande. 'Last time I got so terribly dusty on my way through the attic that it simply wasn't worth it in the end for the tongue-lashing I had off Matron afterwards. She says it's dangerous up there.'

'And it's so dark,' added Rosabelle. 'I'm sure it's haunted. I know the servants don't like going in the attic.

Bessie told me the kitchen-maids hear sounds coming from upstairs sometimes, and they're all convinced there's a ghost.'

'Nonsense,' said Barbara. 'It's probably me they heard. I'll bet if you asked Bessie again she'd tell you they haven't heard a thing since I stopped going up. It's a pity,' she went on wistfully. 'It's the perfect sort of day for sitting on the roof and enjoying the view. But I did promise. Besides, I think they locked the door to the outside after I was caught the last time.'

'It serves you right for chucking eggs at people,' said Florrie.

'You know exactly who was responsible for that,' said Barbara. 'And you ought to be thankful that I didn't squeak on any of you.'

'Oh, we are,' Florrie assured her with all the complacency of one who had escaped her proper deserts.

The group fell silent, munching, until a man walked past, pushing a wheelbarrow. He had an unprepossessing, taciturn air about him.

'Who's that?' said Melisande.

'I don't know,' said Isabel. 'The new gardener, I suppose. He's a bit grumpy-looking, don't you think?'

'He is rather,' said Violet. 'I spoke to him the other day and I could hardly get a reply out of him. He's not as friendly as old Mr. Hill was, at any rate.'

'Perhaps he's a foreign spy, come to kidnap Irina,' said Barbara.

Irina looked up.

'Why do you say that?' she said quickly.

'I don't know,' said Barbara. 'It just came into my head. He looks the sort.'

'Know many foreign spies, do you?' said Florrie impatiently.

'Of course not,' said Barbara.

'Well, then,' said Florrie. 'Better keep your mouth shut, don't you think?'

'There's no need to jump down my throat,' said Barbara.

'Yes there is—you're scaring Irina,' said Florrie, and Barbara now saw that Irina was indeed wearing a frightened expression. 'You oughtn't to joke about that kind of thing.'

'Sorry, Irina,' said Barbara. 'I didn't mean to put the wind up you.'

The bell rang for lessons and the girls all jumped up. Irina hurried off and Florrie ran to catch up with her.

'What was all that about?' said Barbara, as she watched them go. 'Is she really worried about being kidnapped?'

But nobody seemed inclined to answer, so she shrugged, gathered up her things, and headed off to her lesson.

Chapter Six

WHILE BARBARA and her friends were talking on the grass, Angela was on her way to Wakeley Court to fulfil her engagement with Miss Bell, who had promised to show her around the place, introduce her to the teachers, and point out Violet Smedley, the likely (or certain) beneficiary of Angela's generosity. Mrs. Marchmont was to be accommodated in one of the well-appointed rooms the school used for guests, and was to be given every attention. Angela had resigned herself to doing whatever Miss Bell wanted, since that seemed the easiest course, and had also accepted the headmistress's invitation to remain at the school for the weekend, for true to her resolution she had promised to take Barbara out. In fulfilment of her agreement with Henry Jameson, Angela also intended to speak to some of the girls—especially the Princess, whom Barbara had mentioned casually in her latest letter as a new friend— and try to get a sense of what, if anything, was going on at Wakeley Court.

The journey from London was rapid, but after King's Lynn the roads became narrower and the countryside more attractive, and so the Bentley slowed down and proceeded at a stately pace, for the day was a pleasant one.

'By the way, William,' said Angela to her driver. 'While we are at the school I should like you to keep an eye out for suspicious goings-on among the servants.'

William was by now well used to unusual requests of this sort from his employer, and showed no surprise other than a brief flicker of his eyebrows.

'Certainly, ma'am,' he said. 'What sort of thing am I to look for?'

'I don't know, exactly,' said Angela. 'I can't give you the whole story—as a matter of fact, strictly speaking I oughtn't to be telling you this at all, so understand that none of it must go any further. Let us just say, however, that there is an important person at Wakeley Court whose life may be in danger.'

'I see,' said William. 'Do you mean one of the pupils?'

'Yes,' said Angela. 'She is a princess from one of those excitable countries that like to amuse themselves by assassinating their rulers every so often, and I gather there is a threat to her life at present. Someone is already stationed here to protect her, and I have promised to nose about a bit myself, but of course you are much better placed than I to find things out from the servants. Listen to the gossip and see what you can pick up. Perhaps they have seen somebody suspicious hanging about the place, for example. I leave it to you.'

'I'll do my best, ma'am,' said William.

Some little time later they arrived at Wakeley Court. The Bentley drew up in front of the building, which was a handsome one of red brick built in the Gothic revival style, but tastefully so, with a minimum of turrets and decorative tracery. There was a portico running along the front, under which was an arch leading through to the Quad, and the whole building was surrounded by well-kept lawns, although the lake could not be seen from this side. The school was only two or three miles from the sea, and when she stepped out of the car Angela detected a whiff of salt in the air, which she had not noticed on her previous visit.

The place was silent, seemingly deserted, but not for long: William was just unloading the bags when a bell rang loudly, and within seconds the whole place was a sea of girls swarming in every direction, shrieking and giggling, dropping things, jostling one another and waving books about. The noise was deafening, and William looked slightly nervous.

'Angela!' came a voice, and they turned to see Barbara running towards them in company with another girl. 'You're here at last,' she said. 'Splendid. I've just been telling the girls you were coming. You can meet them later.'

'Of course,' said Angela. 'But first I must go and do my duty to the headmistress. She has invited me to have tea with her and some of the teachers.'

'Be sure and put a word in for me with Miss Finch,' said Barbara. 'She was pretty scathing about my History essay earlier. You might tell her I'm a misunderstood genius. Come on, Flo. We'd better go or we'll be late.'

She dashed off, followed by the other girl, leaving Angela to find her own way to the headmistress's room. Miss Bell greeted her with the utmost politeness, and after an exchange of pleasantries escorted her along to the staff common-room, where they were to have tea and Angela was to meet the teachers.

'This is Miss Finch, our Classics and History mistress,' said Miss Bell, introducing a small, dark woman with shrewd eyes and a brisk manner, who looked Angela over with some appearance of misgiving, although whether she had taken a personal dislike to the visitor or whether that was her usual manner was impossible to say. 'She is my deputy.'

'I'm very pleased to meet you,' said Angela.

'You are the godmother of Barbara Wells,' said Miss Finch, and it came out like a snap. 'Bright child, but needs taking in hand. I've seen it before with motherless girls. They can grow up to be quite a handful if not kept in check.'

'Oh yes?' murmured Angela politely.

Miss Bell interjected diplomatically.

'I must say that Barbara has improved tremendously since our little—er—chat two weeks ago,' she said.

Miss Finch nodded, and Miss Bell steered Angela across to another teacher, a small, shrivelled-looking elderly man who sported a splendid, bushy moustache that appeared to have emerged accidentally from his nose and spread across half his face.

'This is Mr. Penkridge, our Music master,' she said. 'Mr. Penkridge, this is Mrs. Marchmont, who has been so generous as to establish the Mathematics scholarship which I mentioned to you the other day.'

Mr. Penkridge gave a little bow and beamed.

'N-hem! Enchanted, madam,' he said. 'I am delighted to hear of your interest in expanding the knowledge of our young minds here. It is only a pity that we did not meet earlier, or I might have persuaded you to extend your philanthropy in the direction of our Music students too.'

'Now, Mr. Penkridge,' said Miss Bell, with some slight embarrassment. 'It will not do to test the generosity of our patrons.' She turned to Angela. 'Mr. Penkridge's enthusiasm occasionally runs away with him, but I assure you that he has nothing but his pupils' best interests at heart.'

'Oh, yes,' said Mr. Penkridge happily. 'Miss Bell will tell you of my firm belief that Music is quite the most important of all subjects. I always say, Mrs. Marchmont, that a life lived without music is a life tragically wasted. One could not say the same of Geography or French, don't you agree? The other teachers laugh at me for my conviction. It is quite a little joke between us. N-hem! And so you are Barbara's godmother?' His smile faltered, but only briefly. 'I don't know whether she has mentioned it to you, but we have been studying Baroque choral music this term, and I may say truthfully of her voice that I have never before encountered one of such volume or penetration.' He paused to reflect briefly. 'No, in all my years of teaching Music I have never heard anything to equal it. Her enthusiasm is quite heartening.'

Having heard Barbara sing once or twice, Angela forbore to put him in an awkward position by questioning him more closely on the subject of her god-daughter's musical abilities, and they moved on to the next teacher. Miss Devlin taught Games and Geography, and greeted Angela with a hearty handshake. A strongly-built woman, as one might expect, she had a surprisingly high, soft voice and a marked speech impediment, which when set against her appearance had an unfortunately comical effect. She said what was proper and then retreated behind her tea-cup.

'This is Mlle. Delacroix,' said Miss Bell, next.

Mam'selle was tall and elegant, and dressed with impeccable Parisian taste, which must have taken some skill and effort on a teacher's salary, thought Angela. The French mistress had a pleasant and humorous manner, and the two ladies hit it off immediately, each perhaps sensing a kindred spirit in the other.

'I like your Barbara,' said Mam'selle. 'Her French is quite dreadful but she is very funny and so I forgive her much.' She glanced over at Miss Bell, who was talking to

Miss Finch at that moment, and lowered her voice. '*She* likes Barbara too, but she will never say it, as it does not do to show favouritism. That is why she did not expel her.'

'Miss Bell seems a very capable woman,' Angela said cautiously.

'Oh, she is,' agreed Mam'selle. 'And as you have found out, she is particularly good at persuading people to part with their money for the good of the school.'

'That's true enough,' said Angela with feeling, and they both laughed.

The next teacher was Mr. Welland.

'Augustus Welland,' he said, introducing himself. The English master was tall and handsome, and evidently very pleased with the fact. He shook back the long lock of hair that fell carelessly over his forehead, and began to talk. Within a very few seconds it became clear that Mr. Welland's chief interest in life was Mr. Welland. Every question he asked Mrs. Marchmont was used merely as a spur from which to introduce some anecdote of his own about himself. Occasionally, he diverged into observations about the wider world, but always he returned to his favourite topic. Within ten minutes, Angela had heard his views upon literature, art, foreign travel (he had recently visited Russia and had many things to say on developments in that country), the Plight of the Working Man, and the trial of the carpenter in Dagenham who murdered all three of his wives and made their coffins himself—all with regard to the way in which they affected him personally. He was just launching into an impassioned diatribe against the professor at his old university who had failed to recognize his genius and award him a double first, when Miss Bell came to the rescue, somewhat to Angela's relief.

She then spoke briefly to Mr. Hesketh, whose

demeanour was as bland as ever and gave no clue as to his real identity or purpose in coming to the school.

'I think the only person you have not yet met is Miss Fazackerley, our Mathematics teacher,' said Miss Bell. 'Barbara no longer has lessons with her, as she and some of the other brighter girls are at present receiving special tuition from me until we can find a suitable teacher—' she looked around. 'Oh, I'm sure she was here a moment ago.'

Angela remembered having seen a lumpish-looking woman with untidy hair and a morose expression, but could not see her now.

'She went out a few minutes ago,' said Mlle. Delacroix.

'Oh dear,' said Miss Bell. 'Then you shall meet her later, Mrs. Marchmont. Mam'selle, will you please show our guest up to her room?'

'Certainly,' said Mam'selle, and stood back politely to let Angela go first. As they left the room, Mr. Hesketh caught Angela's eye then looked away quickly.

The guest-room was a small one, comfortably furnished and with a pretty flowered bedspread and cushion covers which had presumably been made by the girls. Its little window looked out towards one edge of the lake and the tennis courts. Beyond that was a small summer-house and a little way off to one side were some outbuildings.

'It's very pleasant,' said Angela.

'Yes,' said Mam'selle. 'It is not a bad place. English girls are quite impossible, of course, but I am used to them and don't mind them.'

'Have you lived in England long?' said Angela.

'Seven years,' said Mam'selle. 'Although I have been at this school only a year. Before that I was at a school in Yorkshire.'

'Forgive me,' said Angela, 'but you don't look much like

a teacher.'

'No,' admitted the other. 'It was not what was planned for me. My family wanted me to marry a man who was very rich but much older than I, and for a while I believed I could do it.'

'But you preferred teaching?'

'Not exactly,' said Mam'selle. 'I merely decided that I did not wish to marry, so instead of coming to the church I ran away to England.'

'What, on your wedding day?' said Angela, taken aback.

'Yes,' said Mam'selle.

'But what did your family say about it?'

'I don't know,' said Mam'selle with a shrug. 'I have never spoken to them since. Perhaps they are still there at the church, waiting.'

Evidently there was much more to the story than Mam'selle had told, but it would have been rude to inquire, and so Angela remained silent. The French mistress said that she would leave Mrs. Marchmont to arrange herself, and that she must ask if she wanted anything, and then left.

Angela stood by the window looking out at the grounds, and thought that a girls' school seemed a very unlikely place for international intrigue—although, of course, anyone with wicked intentions would hardly go around proclaiming it publicly. Still, the place was peaceful enough at present. She spent a few minutes considering how best to approach her task, and decided to abide by her original plan, which had been to get an introduction to the Princess through Barbara, and see what she could find out from her. It suddenly struck her that Henry Jameson had not said whether or not Princess Irina was aware that a man had been placed at the school for her protection. Did she know about Mr. Hesketh? And, moreover, was Angela permitted to tell Irina that she had also been sent to investigate? Angela did not know, but it was clear that the only way to find out was to speak to Mr. Hesketh, and she resolved to do that as soon as possible.

Dinner would not be for a little while yet, and Miss Bell had invited her to make free of the place and take a stroll around the grounds if she liked, so Angela went downstairs and, after getting lost once or twice, finally found herself in the entrance-hall and went out through the open door. She walked along under the portico and back through another arch, and found herself in the Quad, a lawned courtyard with paths that ran diagonally across from each corner to meet a stone fountain in the centre. Another portico ran all the way around it, and at the edge of the grass stone benches were placed, on which girls might sit and reflect quietly on the beautiful surroundings should they so desire —although given the noise that usually echoed around the walls, it was doubtful whether the benches were ever put to their intended use. The Gothic style was more evident here and the portico made Angela think of cloisters in a convent or a monastery. She half-expected to see nuns walking about the place in pairs, but instead there were only one or two girls in blue and brown tunics, hurrying from one part of the school to another.

After admiring the building for some time, Angela turned and left the Quad the way she had come. As she emerged onto the lawn she was not entirely surprised to see Mr. Hesketh hovering some little distance away. He glanced about as she approached him.

'I take it you wish to speak to me,' said Angela.

'If you don't mind,' he said.

'Where can we go so as not to be overheard?'

'I think we had better remain in the open and make it

look as though I am showing you around the place,' said Hesketh. 'I always find that skulking furtively in corners tends to attract attention, especially in a place such as this,' he explained with a smile.

'I imagine it does,' said Angela. 'Then suppose you show me how delightful and harmonious the school building looks from the lake.'

'It is a nice building, isn't it?' said Hesketh as they walked. 'I rather like it myself. It reminds me of my old school, although I haven't been back to the place in some years.'

They stopped close to the lake and turned back, apparently engaged in gazing at the building.

'So, then, I gather you have been stationed here to protect Princess Irina,' said Angela. 'Teaching at a girls' school must be a quiet life for an Intelligence man.'

'A quiet life, do you call it?' he said. 'I take it you have never taught.'

'No,' admitted Angela.

'Then believe me when I say that I am finding the work quite as lively as anything I have done up to now,' he said with some feeling.

Angela laughed, and he immediately retreated behind his bland manner once again.

'Yes, Mrs. Marchmont,' he continued, 'I have been sent here to keep an eye on things—as, I gather, have you.'

'I have,' she replied. 'Mr. Jameson seemed to think I should be able to find out more from the girls than you can, but I'm not entirely sure what it is I'm supposed to be looking for.'

'I'm not certain myself,' said Hesketh. 'Of course, the most obvious thing is the arrival of any suspicious strangers in the area. My lodgings are in the village, which is about half a mile away, and I have been most fortunate in my landlady, who is a gossip of the highest order and can be relied upon absolutely to report the arrival of anybody new or mysterious—the more mysterious the better, in fact, for she appears to subsist on a diet of penny-dreadfuls and is generally inclined to see spies and murderers wherever she looks. She is also friends with the cook at the school, and quite frequently knows more about what is going on than I do.'

'Goodness,' said Angela. 'I wonder they bothered sending you at all when they might have recruited her instead.'

'The thought had occurred to me,' he said. 'Still, she is not "on the spot," as I am, and so cannot see everything. Of course, you will have realized, Mrs. Marchmont, that the difficulty is not so much the presence of mysterious strangers, as the possibility that someone at the school may be working on behalf of Princess Irina's enemies.'

'Do you think that is the case, then?'

'I can't say for certain,' he said. 'As you have seen for yourself, everything here seems pretty quiet and the teachers above suspicion, and yet my nose tells me that *something* is afoot. I only wish I knew what it was, but I have the impression that somebody is hiding something. It's nothing I can put my finger on, but the last time I had this feeling, the President of a certain country was shortly afterwards deposed and disposed of.'

'Do you suspect one of the teachers? Or perhaps a servant?' said Angela.

He nodded.

'Yes, I think it must be one of the staff,' he replied. 'Miss Bell, who of course knows who I am, has given me as much information as she could about the people who work here, but so far we haven't come up with anything useful. There is one gardener who started here recently about whom we know very little, but Miss Bell assures me that he came with impeccable references.'

'Does Miss Bell take the threat seriously?'

'As seriously as a woman of her type can,' he said, considering. 'I suspect she thinks the whole thing is rather exaggerated. Still, she has promised to keep it quiet.'

'Does the Princess know who you are?' said Angela.

'Yes,' said Hesketh. 'She knows of the threat to her, and that I am here to protect her.'

'You can't protect her all the time, though, if you're living in the village,' said Angela.

'No,' he said, 'and that's the worst of it. I am not strictly permitted to be in the building after seven o'clock. I should, of course, ignore the rules if necessary, but how am I to know when it *is* necessary? If there were to be an attempt on Princess Irina in the middle of the night, for example, then I should be quite useless in a house half a mile away. It is most unsatisfactory.'

Something in his tone suggested to Angela that there had been a little disagreement with Miss Bell on this matter.

'Well, I am staying at the school for the next three nights, so I shall do what I can,' she said.

'Yes, and I am glad of it,' said Hesketh, 'because the whole thing makes me very uncomfortable.' He coughed and glanced about. 'Jameson said he advised you to bring a gun,' he said quietly.

'He did,' replied Angela. 'And I have. Not that I expect I'll need it. As a matter of fact, I rather hope I don't. It doesn't do to be waving guns around in a school full of easily excitable girls.'

'That's true enough,' he said. 'Still, I suggest you keep it with you as much as you can.'

'I shall,' Angela assured him.

Chapter Seven

Dinner was early at Wakeley Court, and Angela sat at the top table with the teachers and renewed her acquaintance with the peculiarities of school food. Afterwards, the girls were free until bed-time, provided they had done their prep, and as the great dining-room emptied Barbara rushed across to Angela and grabbed her arm.

'Come and meet my pals,' she said.

They walked around the building and passed William, who was under the bonnet of the Bentley and had attracted followers in the form of two of the smaller girls, identical twins, who were holding spanners and rags for him and asking him questions. They seemed fascinated by what he had to say.

'They're waiting for us in the Quad,' said Barbara.

Sure enough, in the Quad they found a small group of girls sitting on one of the stone benches.

'Where are the others?' said Barbara.

'Doing their Geography prep,' said Violet Smedley. 'They didn't finish it before dinner because they went to play tennis.'

'Rotten of them,' said Barbara. 'Oh, well. This is my godmother, Angela Marchmont,' she went on, waving a hand carelessly. 'I told you all about her. Angela—Violet Smedley, Florrie Evans, Irina Ivanovitch.'

'It's Ivanoveti,' said Florrie before Irina could speak.

'Sorry,' said Barbara.

Angela regarded Irina with covert interest. The Princess was tall and dark and looked rather older than her years. Her manner was self-contained—sullen, even, although she was polite enough and replied to Angela's pleasantries in careful English. She had a slightly wary look about her—no bad thing, Angela supposed, and only to be expected if she knew her life was in danger.

Barbara suggested they take a walk around the building. They could not go far, she said, as it was getting dark and soon they would have to go inside. Barbara walked on one side of Angela and Violet on the other, and Angela was pleased to find that Violet seemed a very nice girl, if a little staid, and had excellent manners. Florrie and Irina followed behind.

As they completed their circuit of the building they saw William again. The twins were still there with him, peering into the engine with great interest.

'Hallo, William,' said Barbara grandly. 'Are these kids bothering you?'

'Not at all,' he replied. 'As a matter of fact, they're being very helpful.'

'He's been showing us how to fix it,' said one twin, a girl of about eleven, who appeared to have smeared oil all over her face in her excitement.

'So I see,' said Barbara. 'You'll be in for it when Matron sees you. You'd better go back and wash. You're filthy.'

'You're a fine one to talk,' said the girl boldly. 'You've got ink all over your hands and some on your nose, too.'

Before Barbara could tell her off, a bell rang for early bed-time, and the two younger girls ran away, laughing.

'Well!' said Barbara. 'Just wait until I see her again. It's simply not done to cheek a bigger girl.'

'You do it yourself all the time,' Florrie pointed out.

'That's different,' said Barbara. 'I say, though, it must be useful being a twin, don't you think? I mean to say, they can do one another's detentions. I wish I had someone who could pretend to be me when I needed it.'

'Yes, but what if one of you was very very good and the other was very very bad?' said Florrie. 'It seems rather unfair on the good twin to have to take the bad twin's punishments.'

'Oh, I dare say some agreement might be reached,' said Barbara vaguely. 'A financial agreement, I mean.'

Angela happened to glance at Irina while this exchange was going on, and to her utter astonishment saw that the girl was regarding William from under her eyelashes in a way that was quite unmistakable. William had evidently seen it too, for a touch of pink tinged his cheeks and he did not seem to know where to look. In the end he settled for staring at the ground.

'We'd better go back in,' said Violet at last. 'It's nearly dark and we don't want to get a black mark from Miss Finch.'

Barbara snorted but did not argue, and the girls moved off. Angela remained behind for a moment with William.

'Keep an eye on the new gardener,' she said quietly. 'I don't know his name.'

'It's Edwards, ma'am,' said William.

'Goodness, that was fast work!' said Angela. 'We've only been here three hours.'

'The kitchen-maids were talking about him. They don't like him much,' said William.

'Why not?'

'He stares at them through the window when they're working,' he said. 'And he doesn't talk to anyone.'

'Hmm,' said Angela. 'I wonder if Edwards is his real name, or even if he's English. You might try and get him in conversation, and see if you can find out.'

'Certainly, ma'am,' said William. He looked about him. 'Funny—it's difficult to think of something happening in this out-of-the-way place. And I haven't seen anyone yet who looks at all like a princess. I wonder which one she is.'

'You've just met her,' said Angela. 'She's the tall girl with the dark hair who was here with Barbara just now.'

William's face was such a picture that Angela had to turn away and bite her lip hard to avoid laughing out loud.

'Yes,' she went on, once she had regained command of herself. 'She is Princess Irina, the only daughter of Grand Duke Feodor of Morania, and first in line to the throne of that country. Rather an *interesting* young lady, don't you think?'

'I'll say,' was all William could manage.

Angela went on, 'Girls from these foreign countries grow up rather more quickly than English ones, I understand.'

'Is that so?' said William, recovering himself.

'Yes,' said Angela. She paused. 'I'm sure I don't need to remind you to be very careful, William,' she said lightly. 'There is more than one kind of danger.'

'Yes, ma'am,' said William.

'Now, don't forget to see what you can find out about Edwards.'

'No, ma'am,' said William.

Angela bade him goodnight and walked off, leaving

William staring at the Bentley and rubbing his head in some perplexity.

Friday morning was spent in discussing formal arrangements for the Mathematics scholarship with Miss Bell and three of the trustees, worthy-looking gentleman to a man, and with conversation to match. At lunch-time Angela was set free, much to her relief, and went to the dining-room to endure more of the school's hearty fare.

In the afternoon, Miss Bell insisted on escorting her around the school to see the girls at work. Angela was taken to see the Fifth Form as they received a Classics lesson from the stern Miss Finch. The class was quiet and studious—Miss Finch evidently had no trouble in keeping order—and Miss Bell nodded approvingly. Irina and Florrie looked up and smiled when they saw Angela, who was slightly surprised, for she had assumed they were in the Fourth with Barbara. Then she remembered that Henry Jameson had spoken of Irina as being almost sixteen— which perhaps went some way to explaining the girl's apparent maturity in other respects.

They then looked in on Miss Devlin's Geography lesson with the Fourth, and there found quite a different atmosphere, for despite her imposing build, Miss Devlin was clearly known to the girls as an easy mark. When Miss Bell opened the door they were greeted by the noise of twenty girls all chattering at once, and the first thing Angela saw was Barbara in the very act of tying a knot in the long pigtail of the unsuspecting girl sitting in front of her. The room fell silent as Miss Bell entered, and Barbara sat back hurriedly after receiving a glare from Angela.

'Quiet, please, girls,' said Miss Bell stiffly, and Miss Devlin looked flustered.

'Yes, quiet please,' she said. 'I have already told you several times.'

Miss Bell and Angela went out and Angela immediately heard the noise begin again.

'Miss Devlin is a good teacher in many respects,' said Miss Bell, 'but I am afraid she finds the discipline side of things a little difficult—in the classroom at least. She also teaches Games, however, and her manner when instructing the girls in physical exercise is quite different. She becomes quite a different woman then—as you will see shortly, when we go to watch the Games lesson, which is next.'

Miss Bell was quite right, for some time later Angela found herself wincing a little as she stood at the edge of the lacrosse field and watched the Games mistress tearing about and shrieking orders to the players.

'It is so good for the girls to spend time racing around in the open air, getting up a nice, healthy perspiration,' said Miss Devlin, running up to Angela, her face glowing and her hair curling up in damp wisps. 'I do it myself as often as I can. There's nothing quite like it.'

'Oh, I agree with you entirely,' said Angela, cool and immaculate under her parasol.

'If you will excuse me,' said Miss Bell, 'I am expecting a visit from the parents of a prospective new girl shortly, and I dislike keeping my visitors waiting.'

She went off, and Angela, for want of anything better to do, remained to watch the lesson. It was the Fourth again, and Miss Devlin appeared to be getting her revenge for their inattention during Geography, for she did not let them rest for a second. During a particularly lively point in the game, one girl dropped her lacrosse stick and tripped over it, and sat, nursing her knee in pain. Miss Devlin rushed over to see to her, and while her attention was distracted, Angela saw a sly-looking girl she had not noticed before hit Barbara hard on the shin deliberately with her lacrosse stick. Barbara yelped, and was just about to retaliate when she spotted Angela and changed her mind. Instead, she moved away from the girl. Angela smiled approvingly. Miss Devlin returned, having patched up the injured girl to her satisfaction, and the game recommenced. Angela did her best to pay attention, but lacrosse had never been a favourite game of hers and so she found her attention wandering.

'Is that Miss Fazackerley?' she said suddenly, as she spotted a woman hurrying towards the outbuildings near the summer-house. Beyond that was a path which was a short-cut out of the school grounds.

Miss Devlin glanced in the direction in which Angela was looking.

'Yes,' she said. 'Whatever can she be doing? She's not supposed to go out during school time.'

'Perhaps she needs to post a letter urgently,' suggested Angela.

'I don't see what can be so urgent at this time of day,' said Miss Devlin. 'The last post is not until six.'

'That reminds me, I have business at the post-office myself,' said Angela. 'You don't suppose Miss Bell would mind if I just ran into the village, do you?'

'No, I don't suppose so,' said Miss Devlin, who was only half-listening. 'Foul!' she bellowed suddenly, and blew her whistle.

Angela needed no further encouragement. She left the girls to their exercise and set off in pursuit of Miss Fazackerley.

Chapter Eight

THE PATH behind the summer-house led through a little wood and out on to the road into the village. Angela had decided that there was no sense in trying to be too secretive, as she was far too easy to spot in her pale-blue frock, and in any case she had a perfectly good excuse for following Miss Fazackerley if that lady did happen to catch sight of her, since this was the quickest way into the village. Of course, there might be a perfectly innocent reason why the Maths mistress was breaking rules and leaving the school grounds when she ought not, but then again there might not, and Angela *had* promised to keep her eyes open, after all.

Miss Fazackerley hurried on without looking behind her, and Angela followed, not too quickly. At length they came to the village and Miss Fazackerley began to walk faster. She passed the post-office, thus disproving Angela's idle surmise, and seemed to be heading for the church, but before she got there she suddenly turned right into a narrow lane and disappeared. Angela halted at the bottom of the lane and looked up it, but there was no sign of Miss

Fazackerley. She entered the lane and proceeded cautiously; if she were to be spotted now she had no good excuse at all for being where she was, for there was nothing up here but one or two dilapidated old barns—and in fact the road came to a dead-end a hundred yards further up.

She walked up the lane slowly, glancing about her as she did so. A low wall bounded the road to the left and right. It was broken in places, but there was nothing on the other side except long grass and weeds. Miss Fazackerley must have gone into one of the barns, then. This was starting to look very suspicious indeed. Angela came to the first one. Its door was wide open, and she could hear the murmur of voices coming from within. Obviously it would be folly to walk straight in, so she tiptoed as stealthily as she could around the building, looking for holes in the planking through which she might listen. She found a knot-hole at the back and peered through it but could see nothing. Then she tried to listen. She could still hear the voices, but they were no clearer. There seemed to be two of them: a woman and a man. Presumably the woman was Miss Fazackerley, but who was the man?

The voices continued talking for a few minutes and Angela began to feel a little silly, standing there listening. What if someone came and found her skulking behind the barn? She had almost decided to creep away quietly when the woman's voice was suddenly raised, and Angela heard quite clearly the words:

'Look here, I've told you: I'll do what I can, but I can't promise anything more, so please stop asking.'

The voices then faded to a murmur again, and shortly afterwards Angela heard footsteps. She peered cautiously around the corner and saw Miss Fazackerley coming out of the barn, looking cross and upset. The teacher strode off down the lane and Angela waited to see who the man was. He emerged shortly afterwards—a shifty-looking specimen who walked with his shoulders hunched up and his hands in his pockets. He followed after Miss Fazackerley, and Angela was left to wonder what it was all about.

She waited a minute or two until the coast was clear and then set off back in the direction of the high street. She had not gone more than a few yards, however, when a thought struck her and she turned back and entered the barn itself. The place seemed almost dark after the glare of the day, but her eyes very quickly became accustomed to the gloom and she glanced around. There was very little to see: just a few bits of rusty machinery and a leaky pail or two, but her eyes soon fastened on what she had been seeking, for over in the darkest, least draughty corner of the barn, next to an old farm cart with a broken wheel, were the unmistakable signs that someone had been using the place to sleep in. Angela went across and regarded the makeshift bed of blankets and the old rolled-up mackintosh which formed a pillow. Presumably the man to whom Miss Fazackerley had been talking was sleeping here, then. She frowned and peered more closely at the blankets. Yes, there was no doubt of it: they were from Wakeley Court. There was the familiar 'W. C.' monogram which caused the girls such endless mirth, and which had prompted even Miss Bell to wonder whether they perhaps ought to have added an S. Had Miss Fazackerley taken the blankets to give to the man? It seemed a reasonable assumption. But who was he? Had he anything to do with the assassination plot? Angela resolved to speak to Mr. Hesketh as soon as she could and advise him to find out whether Miss Fazackerley was known to have any connections with Morania. Hesketh had said he was looking for suspicious people in the area, and this man seemed to fit the description perfectly.

Angela left the barn and returned to the high street. She had just emerged from the lane when she saw Miss Fazackerley herself just coming out of a nearby shop. Miss Fazackerley saw her at the same time, and her eyes widened. She must be wondering what Angela had been doing in the lane. Feeling the need to carry the situation off with aplomb, Angela went across to her boldly and said with her most charming smile:

'Hallo, it's Miss Fazackerley, isn't it? I'm sorry we didn't have the chance to be introduced yesterday. I understand you have done wonders with my god-daughter, Barbara Wells.'

She understood no such thing, but Miss Fazackerley looked uncertain, and muttered something politely.

Angela glanced about her in apparent distraction.

'I was looking for the post-office, as I wanted to send a telegram,' she went on, 'but I'm afraid I got rather lost and ended up in that lane there.'

'The post-office is just behind you,' said Miss Fazackerley.

Angela glanced around.

'Oh! So it is,' she said. 'How on earth did I miss it? I mustn't have been paying attention. Thank you.'

She turned away, but Miss Fazackerley, clearly still suspicious, said, 'I am going to the post-office too,' and so Angela had no choice but to go with her.

A few minutes later they emerged (Angela thinking with some little satisfaction of Marthe's puzzled face when she received a telegram which read, '*Please ignore this telegram*') and walked back to Wakeley Court together, since there was no way for either of them to get out of it. Angela tried to make conversation, but it was difficult going, for Miss Fazackerley was an awkward, taciturn sort, and it was no doubt a relief to both of them when they arrived back at the school. Miss Fazackerley hurried off—she had made no mention of the fact that she had broken the rules by leaving the school grounds—and Angela was left to amuse herself. Fortunately, she immediately met Mlle. Delacroix, who invited Angela to her room to take tea, and they spent a pleasant hour talking about things other than school—for Mam'selle was not one of those teachers who had no other topic of conversation, which came as something of a relief to Angela after a whole day of listening to talk of school matters.

Mr. Hesketh was engaged in giving the brighter members of the Third extra Latin tuition, and did not finish until just before dinner-time, so Angela was unable to speak to him immediately. It would have looked odd had she hovered outside the classroom waiting for him, and so she could not prevent him from being button-holed by a very serious-looking Miss Bell as soon as he came out. Angela began to be a little worried that he would leave the school and go home before she could tell him of her adventure that afternoon, and went in to dinner with the thing on her mind. Miss Fazackerley was sitting at the table, attacking her plate with great enthusiasm and seeming totally unconcerned about her mysterious meeting of that afternoon, and Angela began to wonder whether she was making too much of it. Perhaps it was considered normal behaviour here at Wakeley Court to sneak out and meet rough-looking men in barns. But no—of course it was not. Hesketh must be informed, and soon.

Engaged in her own thoughts, Angela was not paying much attention to what was going on in the dining-room, but gradually she became aware that there was some sort of commotion among the girls, and she looked up to see Irina Ivanoveti just leaving the dining-room in company with Miss Finch, while everybody else looked on in surprise. Angela glanced along the teachers' table and noticed that Miss Bell was not there.

'Has something happened?' she asked of Mam'selle, who shrugged.

Certain that something was amiss, Angela pushed away her plate without much regret and hurried along to Miss Bell's study, forgetting for a moment that the headmistress had no idea of why she was really there. She arrived just as Mr. Hesketh was coming out.

'I was just coming to look for you,' he said.

'What is it?' she said.

'Bad news, I'm afraid,' he said soberly. 'We have just received a telegram from Vorgorod to say that there has been an attempt on the life of the Grand Duke Feodor.'

Chapter Nine

'Oh!' exclaimed Angela. 'Then there really *was* a threat. How dreadful. Is he—'

'He is still alive, but gravely wounded,' said Hesketh, 'and it is by no means certain that he will survive.'

'But what happened?'

'He was shot by an unknown assailant this morning while out on his horse,' said Hesketh. 'He was removed to the palace as quickly as possible and is being attended by the best doctors in the country, but it's touch and go, I'm afraid.'

'How terrible,' said Angela. 'Poor Irina. She has been told, I take it?'

He nodded.

'And how is she?'

'She has taken the news very well, considering,' he said. 'She is a royal personage, however, and has been brought up to this sort of thing, odd as it may seem to the rest of us.'

'But if what you say is true, and the Grand Duke really is in such a bad way, then she may very shortly inherit the throne of Morania,' said Angela. 'She will have little time for mourning in that case.'

'She may have no time at all,' said Hesketh grimly. 'There is no saying whether the assassins mayn't have sent someone here to Norfolk too. I am dreadfully worried that Princess Irina's life may be in imminent danger.'

'Then what can be done to protect her?'

'I have already told Miss Bell that there is no question of my going back to the village tonight,' he said, 'and she has been forced to accept it. In addition, we have received a telegram from the Princess's cousin, Count Paul, who has assumed temporary authority in the country, to say that he has sent the head of the Moranian Intelligence service to England, and this man will arrive tomorrow. It was this Everich who discovered the original assassination plot, and so he will no doubt be able to tell us more about the sort of people we must look out for.'

Angela suddenly remembered why she had originally wanted to speak to him, and quickly told him of her adventure of the afternoon. He listened in surprise, then seemed to be considering.

'That is news to me,' he said, 'and rather worrying. Should you be able to recognize this man again if you saw him?'

'I think so,' said Angela. 'He was fairly distinctive. And we know where to find him, anyway. He is sleeping in the barn.'

'Yes. We shall have to be vigilant,' said Hesketh. 'I shall make sure the staff are warned to keep an eye out for any man matching his description, and not to let him enter the school grounds.'

'But what about Miss Fazackerley?' said Angela. 'If she is in league with this man, then she is presumably a danger. Why, she might let him into the school when everybody is asleep. Oughtn't we to let her know at least that we suspect her?'

'I'm not certain that is a good idea,' he said. 'If we put her on her guard, then she might warn the man and he will get away.'

'But we can catch him now,' said Angela. 'We know where he is.'

'And accuse him of what, exactly?' said Hesketh. 'As far as we know, he hasn't done anything. If we go and speak to him now, he will move on, perhaps to a better hiding-place.'

'But does that matter? After all, surely the most important thing is that Princess Irina be kept safe from harm.'

'It is indeed,' said Hesketh, 'and I think we can do that without difficulty for the moment, without needing to warn her enemies that we suspect them. Miss Bell has agreed that tonight the Princess will share her room. They are taking up a spare bed now, in fact. Irina will go to bed at the usual time and lock herself in, and when Miss Bell comes up to bed she will give a knock in code, so that Irina knows it is safe to admit her. Tomorrow we will speak to this Everich fellow and see what he can tell us. Perhaps he knows something of the man you saw. We shall also question Miss Fazackerley if necessary.'

'Wouldn't it be better to do that tonight?' said Angela, who privately thought that Hesketh was being unnecessarily circumspect now that the danger had proved to be real.

'Perhaps,' he said. 'But don't forget, Mrs. Marchmont, that we are still under orders to keep this whole thing as secret as possible. Think of the panic it would cause if we started accusing the teachers of plotting to assassinate one of the girls. No,' he went on, 'the fewer people who know of this, the better.'

'Then is there anything I can do?' said Angela.

'You might keep an eye on Miss Fazackerley yourself, if you like,' he replied. He saw her face and laughed. 'You think me guilty of inactivity, Mrs. Marchmont,' he said. 'I assure you I am doing everything I can, but there is only one of me, and there is no sense in my haring about the countryside looking for mysterious men when the person who is their target is here at the school. My job is to protect the Princess, and for that I need to be here.'

There was no arguing with that, and so Angela was forced to be content with returning to the staff common-room, where she spent the evening pretending not to watch Miss Fazackerley, who spent two perfectly innocent hours marking papers and then went to bed at nine o'clock. There was little to do after that, since most of the teachers tended to retire early, and so Angela followed suit shortly afterwards.

On Saturday morning Angela went down to breakfast and immediately saw that Miss Fazackerley was missing. She glanced quickly over towards the girls' tables and to her relief saw Irina, safe and well, toying with her breakfast, pale in the face and deep in thought.

'Where is Miss Fazackerley?' she said to Miss Devlin.

'She went off to catch the early train,' said Miss Devlin. 'Her mother is elderly and infirm, and Miss Bell allows her to spend the whole weekend away from the school every other week.'

'Oh!' said Angela, wondering whether Mr. Hesketh knew about it. He might have thought differently about questioning Miss Fazackerley the night before had he known she was to be absent today. Still, at least she was safely off the premises for now, and would thus be unable to admit any would-be assassins in the dead of night.

After breakfast Angela went to find Barbara, for she

had promised to take her out. The Moranian Intelligence man was meant to be arriving soon, and so Angela did not suppose that she could be wanted any more.

'There you are,' said Barbara, linking an arm through Angela's. 'Have you heard about poor Irina's father?'

'Yes,' said Angela. 'Has there been any news of his condition?'

'No change,' said Barbara. 'They're sending her telegrams every few hours. She might be an orphan soon, like me,' she said cheerfully.

'Let us hope not,' said Angela.

'No,' said Barbara, more soberly. 'I don't feel it myself since I never knew mine, of course, but I expect it must be pretty rotten to lose one's parents if one happens to be acquainted with them. Her mother died a few years ago, you know, and so she's only got her father. I suppose she'll be sorry to lose him.'

'Besides, if her father does die then Irina will have to return to Morania, as she will inherit the throne,' said Angela.

'I should hate that,' said Barbara. 'If it were I, I'd pay someone to rule for me, and then go off and have lots of larks.'

'I'm not sure you'd be allowed to do that,' said Angela. 'I rather think that sort of thing is frowned upon in those circles. I believe they require one to do at least *some* ruling in return for one's royal privilege.'

'Ugh, how horrid,' said Barbara, then promptly forgot the subject. 'By the way,' she said, 'look at the bruise on my shin. Did you see what the vile Everard female did to me with her lacrosse stick yesterday?'

'I certainly did,' said Angela, 'and I agree she does seem somewhat objectionable. However, I think you would do better to stop referring to her as "the vile Everard female," since it is hardly likely to do anything to improve relations between the two of you, and, moreover, I'm quite certain Miss Finch would not approve.'

Barbara laughed, quite unchastened, and gave Angela's arm an affectionate squeeze, then ran off to get her hat while Angela went to speak to William. He had brought the Bentley around to the front of the building and was standing talking to his two small friends of the other evening.

'Well?' said Angela, once the two girls had been induced with difficulty to go away. 'Have you managed to speak to this Edwards fellow?'

William shook his head.

''Fraid not, ma'am,' he said. 'Lord knows, I've tried, but every time I came anywhere near him he seemed to remember he had to be somewhere else, and hurried off.'

'Dear me!' said Angela. 'That sounds rather suspicious in itself—running away every time someone tries to talk to him.'

'Maybe he didn't like the look of me,' said William, who felt a little guilty at having failed in his mission.

'Impossible,' said Mrs. Marchmont kindly. 'There must have been some other reason. Well, never mind—we shall go out and enjoy ourselves by the seaside today. I don't suppose you've heard, but there have been developments in the case and so I doubt we'll be wanted any more.'

'As a matter of fact, I did hear something about it,' he said.

'I expect you're going to tell me now that the servants know the whole story,' said Angela.

'Pretty much,' admitted William. 'At least, they know that the Princess is thought to be in danger.'

'I don't know why anybody bothers trying to keep secrets at all,' said Angela, as Barbara ran towards them, waving her hat triumphantly. 'Don't say anything to Barbara, by the way, or she'll start tearing about the countryside, looking for assassins.'

They set off along the road in the direction of the sea, heading for the little coastal town of Percham and its ancient harbour, which had long ago ceased to be a working port and was now used only by pleasure-craft and the odd fishing-boat. Although it was a sunny day, the weather had finally turned, and there was a chill in the air that was much more like October than the sticky temperatures of the past fortnight had been. The Bentley proceeded at a leisurely pace along the coast road, from where they had occasional glimpses of sand flats separated by many inlets and channels, which were dotted about with small boats. A little way out, one or two sand banks rose out of the water, and on them enormous flocks of sea-birds could be spied jostling, flapping and soaring into the sky. The air was filled with a salty tang and the views were very fine, and so the journey was a pleasant one.

Percham was only a few miles away, and they reached it in very little time. Barbara had some pocket-money to spend and knew of a particular shop which sold the sorts of things that appealed to girls of her age, and so Angela and Barbara left William with the car and went in to poke about the shop and make impossible requests of the proprietor. Having spent some time amusing themselves in this fashion, they went outside and took a stroll along the front—which was not quite as comfortable as it might have been the day before, given the change in the temperature. Still, they agreed that it was a splendid day, and bore it as long as they could until the chilly breeze forced them to seek shelter and somewhere for lunch. They decided to go to a large hotel which overlooked the harbour and had large windows through which they might enjoy the view in comfort without having to suffer the cold. After some negotiation and a polite refusal to be fobbed off with a back room, Angela and Barbara were shown into the hotel's grand dining-room, and immediately saw that someone had got there before them.

'Hallo, Irina,' said Barbara. 'Whatever are you doing here?'

It was indeed the Princess, who was sitting at a table with a man of unmistakably foreign appearance. He was tall, with hair as pale as straw, a nose that erred towards the Roman, and piercing blue eyes which turned down at the outer corners. His high cheekbones and a certain lift to the chin gave him the look of a nobleman, or perhaps an important military personage, although he was dressed in quite normal clothing.

'Hallo, Barbara,' said Irina without notable enthusiasm, but did not introduce the man. He, however, leapt to his feet, bowed to the two newcomers and said in clipped tones:

'Good day. I am Raul Everich, trusted servant of His Highness the Grand Duke of Morania.'

Angela introduced herself and Barbara and tried not to look at Everich too curiously. He, however, had no such scruples, and regarded the two of them with undisguised interest.

'I am very sorry to hear about your father, Irina,' said Angela. 'Have you heard anything further about his condition?'

'Everich says he is very ill,' said Irina dully.

'I very much fear he is,' said Everich. 'It is too soon to say whether he will recover, although we can but hope. Everyone in Morania is praying for him.'

'Have you caught the people responsible?' said Angela.

'Alas, the attack was sudden and unexpected,' said

Everich. 'We were aware of a plot to assassinate His Highness and had taken steps to protect him, but this attempt came from a completely unexpected quarter. It happened while he was out riding in his own park, and we do not yet know how the assailant or assailants managed to get in, for the boundary walls are very high and impossible to climb over.'

'Goodness,' said Angela. 'That sounds rather to me as though there were a traitor on the inside.'

Everich bowed his head.

'It pains me to doubt the loyalty of His Highness's servants, but I fear you may be right,' he said. 'The Grand Duke's cousin, Count Paul of Vorgorod, has been distraught at the whole affair, and has personally launched an investigation into the tragedy, but that is of little use after the fact. We can do nothing but watch and hope. In the meantime, His Excellency has sent me here to watch over Her Highness and ensure that she remains safe from harm. Now, Your Highness, if you are quite finished, we had better return to the school.'

The two of them left, Everich with another smart bow, and Angela and Barbara were left to order their own lunch. Angela wondered idly why the head of Moranian Intelligence had thought it a good idea to take Irina out of school when she was believed to be in such danger, but supposed that he must have taken his own precautions about which she knew nothing. At any rate, here was an expert in Moranian matters, and if anyone was in a position to spot the threat to the Princess, it was he.

Chapter Ten

THAT EVENING, Angela could not shake off the feeling that something was about to happen. Why she should feel so she did not know, for there were plenty of precautions in place. Even if the mysterious man in the barn *were* loitering with malicious intent, Miss Fazackerley was away at present and unable to admit him into the school. Mr. Everich was here now, and was presumably best placed to know how to protect the Princess—and even if he had not arrived so quickly, Irina was being watched at all times, and her bed had been moved to Miss Bell's room, where she remained safely under lock and key at night. No— there was no particular reason to scent danger, and yet Angela did. Perhaps she had been unconsciously influenced by Mr. Hesketh and Henry Jameson, who had the same unexplained feeling that something was wrong. But they were experienced Intelligence men, and if they sensed trouble, then the feeling was not to be taken lightly, and so Angela was unwilling to dismiss her fears.

She decided to go and have a word with William, and wandered out into the Quad, for that was the quickest way to the building which housed the school charabanc, used to collect girls from the station, and one or two other vehicles. William was bunking in there with the deaf old driver, who had formerly been a coachman and had adapted to motorization without a murmur—indeed, some wag had pointed out that given the way he drove, he had obviously not noticed that someone had taken the horses away. As Angela passed the fountain, she saw Barbara's friends Violet and Florrie sitting together on one of the stone benches. Violet had her head buried in a book, while Florrie was reading a letter. Angela waved, but neither of them saw her.

William was not in the coach-house, but she found him at the back of the building, rubbing an oily rag over something that looked like it might be a part from the Bentley, an unlit cigarette dangling from the corner of his mouth. He removed the cigarette at once when he saw her, but Angela was not thinking about that and glanced at the part.

'Will it go without that?' she said. 'If not, I suggest you put it back in. I don't know why, but I don't quite like the idea of the car's being out of action at the moment.'

'That's all right,' he said. 'It won't take a minute to replace it. Are we expecting trouble, ma'am?'

'Yes—no—I don't know,' she said. 'It's nothing I can put my finger on, and I dare say nobody wants me to meddle in the thing now that the professionals presumably have everything in hand, but obviously given what's happened in Morania, it's of the utmost importance that the Princess be kept safe, and so I feel I ought to be on my guard.'

'Is there anything I can do?' said William, who was all for adventure.

'Not at present, except be vigilant. I might need you

later, but I don't know when. You don't mind a bit of rough stuff, do you?'

'The more the better,' he said enthusiastically.

'Well, don't get too carried away,' she said, amused. 'There's danger about and I don't want anyone to get hurt.'

William's expression clearly indicated what he thought of that.

'I don't suppose you've seen Edwards since you got back?' went on Angela.

'I'm afraid not, ma'am,' he said.

'I didn't expect so,' she said. 'Never mind. He's probably a perfectly respectable man who works hard to support his wife and six children, and I'm maligning him unfairly by suspecting him of evil intent. Now, don't forget to put that part back, and be ready for trouble.'

She went off, intending to look for Mr. Hesketh. It seemed that he was looking for her too, for as soon as she entered the building she found him in the entrance-hall waiting for her, and they went back outside so as not to be overheard.

'I see the Moranian Intelligence man has arrived,' said Angela.

'Oh, you've seen him, have you?' said Hesketh.

'Barbara and I bumped into him and Irina in Percham today,' said Angela.

'I should have preferred it had they stayed at the school,' said Hesketh, 'but I suppose if anyone knows the enemy, he does. He was perfectly confident that the Princess would be safe, and so I didn't feel I could insist.'

'By the way, did you know that Miss Fazackerley has gone away until tomorrow?' said Angela.

'Yes,' said Hesketh. 'I hope that means we have nothing

to fear from her or this man you saw—at least for the moment.'

'Then I suppose you are going to tell me that my services are no longer required,' said Angela.

'On the contrary,' said Hesketh. 'I assume this Everich fellow will want to take the Princess back to Morania in the next day or two, but in the meantime her life is still in danger, so it can't hurt to have as many people as possible keeping an eye out—at least for as long as we are responsible for her.'

'Poor Irina,' said Angela. 'She must be desperate to go home and see her father. What an awful burden to have to bear at fifteen.'

'Yes,' said Hesketh. 'Still, she seems mature for her years and may be able to put up with it better than other girls of her age.'

He then took his leave, and Angela was left standing deep in thought until roused by Barbara, who was looking for Florrie. Angela sent her off to the Quad, then shook herself and went to the staff common-room, there to spend a very dull evening listening to Miss Devlin's plans for coaching the hockey team and winning some inter-school championship or other. The Games mistress's soft tones had a remarkably soporific effect, and after an hour or so Angela was able to say with truth that she was feeling quite sleepy, and escape to her room without fear of seeming rude. There she undressed and got into bed, and after a few futile minutes trying to read, turned off the lamp and went to sleep.

She awoke with a start some time later, and lay for a moment, her heart thumping. What was it that had awoken her? A noise, perhaps? Angela listened for a minute, but could hear nothing. She fumbled for her watch, which lay on the little table by her bed, and was just able to see that it was twenty minutes past two. She was wide awake now and knew she would be unable to get back to sleep, so after a moment's reflection she got out of bed and dressed quickly. She was just about to leave the room when she suddenly remembered something, and turned back to take her little revolver out of a drawer. She slipped it into her pocket then went to the door, opened it cautiously and listened. Outside in the passage she could hear nothing. To her right were the stairs, which led to a downstairs corridor, from where it was a quick run past the staff common-room and through to the rear atrium and the back door. To her left was Miss Bell's room, and a little way past that Miss Devlin's room. Angela knew that Mr. Hesketh was sleeping in one of the guest-rooms at the very end of the passage. Might it have been he she had heard?

Just then, to her right, she heard the unmistakable sound of a stair creaking. It was not very loud, but it sounded almost deafening in the darkness. Angela felt her heart jump into her throat. She paused to catch her breath —and, it must be admitted, to summon up her courage and resist the urge to run back into her room—then took her revolver out of her pocket and crept along to the stairs as quietly as she could. The moon was shining in through a large, arched window opposite the head of the staircase, and rather than step into the full view of anyone who happened to cast a glance backwards, Angela stopped to one side and poked her head around carefully. There was nothing—only empty gloom. After a short flight, the stairs paused at a little landing and then turned to the right and continued out of view, and as Angela listened she was certain she could hear the sound of someone creeping quietly downstairs further ahead.

Feeling the comforting shape of the gun under her hand, Angela took a deep breath, entered the dark mouth of the staircase and began to descend, keeping to the edges in an attempt to avoid the creaky step. At the little landing she paused and peered around the corner. The next flight was longer and led down into absolute blackness. Angela quailed for a second—but only a second. She drew herself up.

'Now, we'll have none of this,' she told herself firmly. 'What sort of a detective are you if you can't even walk down a flight of stairs without going into a blue funk? Why, you might as well go and confess to Mr. Hesketh this minute that you're a useless coward.'

Having fortified herself in this manner, she listened for a moment and then set forth down the next flight. She reached the bottom without incident and paused, straining to see. Gradually her eyes became accustomed to the increased darkness, and she could make out the outline of the door to the staff common-room, which was opposite. She tried the handle carefully but it was locked. Whoever it was must then have gone through the door at the end of the corridor and into the rear atrium. Angela followed, and swiftly discovered that her mysterious quarry had left the door slightly ajar. Warily she opened it and was immediately almost blinded by the moonlight which flooded into the atrium through the large windows. In an instant she saw that the back door was open, and ran towards it. Outside all was quiet, and she stood, gazing out across the lawns, which glowed pale under the moon, but could see nobody. Whoever it was might have gone in any direction —might even be hiding behind a bush or a tree. It was useless to try and search the grounds by herself. She would go and fetch Mr. Hesketh immediately. Perhaps he would know what to do.

She ran back upstairs, past her room and along to the end of the passage, less careful of the noise she was making this time, then knocked on Mr. Hesketh's door. He answered immediately and she was not at all surprised to see that he was fully dressed and wide awake. Quickly, she explained in a whisper what had happened, and his face set into a grim expression.

'You'd better show me,' he said, and shut the door behind him. They had not gone far when he said, 'Wait. I'll go and get my torch,' and turned back.

It was at this point that disaster struck. Miss Devlin, who had been woken up by the sound of Angela hurrying along the passage to fetch Mr. Hesketh, came out of her room to see what was going on just as Mr. Hesketh was passing, and the two of them bumped into one another. Since nobody had informed Miss Devlin that the Latin master was staying there at present, she immediately took it that the strange man with whom she had collided in the dark was a burglar. She shrieked, and for a few seconds the two of them grappled together in the gloom, until Mr. Hesketh managed to free himself and stepped back.

'Oh, no you don't!' cried Miss Devlin. 'Help! Police!'

She accompanied her yell with a neat yet powerful right hook, which connected with Mr. Hesketh's jaw and laid him out flat. As he lay there groaning, Miss Devlin stepped over him and turned on a nearby wall-lamp.

'Why, it's Mr. Hesketh!' she said in astonishment as she looked down at the young man's prostrate figure.

She glanced up and saw Angela standing open-mouthed nearby, and her eyes widened. Despite herself, Angela almost laughed as she quite clearly saw an awful suspicion enter the Games mistress's head, but other concerns swiftly intruded and she ran forward and bent over the unfortunate young man, who was rubbing his jaw groggily and attempting to sit up.

'Are you all right?' said Angela. 'Help me get him up, Miss Devlin.'

'I'm all right, I think,' said Hesketh. He refused her hand and got to his feet slowly.

'But what—' Miss Devlin began, looking from Angela to Mr. Hesketh and back again. 'Why is Mr. Hesketh here? I thought you were a burglar.'

'No, I'm not a burglar,' said Hesketh grimly, moving his head from side to side to make sure it was still attached to his neck. He winced.

It was finally beginning to dawn on Miss Devlin that laying out the Latin master with a single punch was perhaps not the best way to foster good relations with a fellow teacher, and she went pink in the face at the enormity of what she had done.

'Oh, dear me!' she exclaimed. 'Oh, Mr. Hesketh, I'm most dreadfully sorry. How will you ever forgive me? Let me run downstairs and get you some ice.'

'No, no,' said Hesketh.

'Oh, but I insist,' said Miss Devlin. 'It's the least I can do.'

All three of them were by now very embarrassed, but how the situation might eventually have resolved itself will never be known, for at that moment there was an interruption in the form of Miss Bell, who emerged from her room in a hurry, glanced around at them all and said urgently:

'Where is the Princess?'

Chapter Eleven

DESPITE THE PAIN in his jaw, Hesketh was instantly alert.

'What do you mean? Isn't she in there with you?' he said.

'No,' said Miss Bell. 'I woke up and heard a noise out here, and thought she must have left the room for some reason. Where is she?'

'I beg your pardon,' said Mr. Hesketh, and went into Miss Bell's room, followed by the others.

The bedside lamp was switched on, and it was immediately evident that there was no-one in the room. Hesketh looked at the little bed which was Irina's, then bent over and peered under it, but without much hope.

'But how did she get out?' he said. 'You locked the door, I assume, Miss Bell?'

'Of course I did,' she said. 'And I put my keys in my bedside drawer here, as I always do.'

She pulled open the drawer as she spoke. Her mouth opened then closed again.

'Gone,' said Mr. Hesketh, and it was not a question.

Miss Bell nodded wordlessly.

'But why?' said Angela. 'Why did she leave the room of her own accord if she knew she was in danger?'

'I don't know,' said Mr. Hesketh, 'but we had better hurry if we want to catch her.'

He turned to leave the room, and Angela followed him.

'Wait!' said Miss Bell, and went after them in her dressing-gown. Miss Devlin, not understanding at all what was going on, followed.

They all hurried down the stairs and along the corridor to the rear atrium, Miss Bell switching on lights as they went. When they arrived at the back door, they saw what Angela had already seen some time earlier.

'My keys!' exclaimed Miss Bell, as she spied the articles in question dangling from the lock of the door. She took them and put them in her pocket.

'Then there's no doubt,' said Angela. 'Irina took the keys and went out of her own volition.'

The four of them went outside. There was a sharp chill in the air but Miss Bell, awake and capable in her night-things, made no mention of it.

'Which way did she go, do you suppose?' she said.

'I don't know,' said Hesketh. 'Of course, it depends on why she came out. If she came out to meet someone, then the summer-house or one of the outbuildings might be the most likely place. If, on the other hand, she was intending to run away from the school, then she might have gone along the path to the village, or even out through the front gates.'

'She might just be out for mischief,' said Miss Devlin, who knew nothing of the assassination plot. 'Don't you remember, Miss Bell, when the Third took it into their heads to go and play tennis at midnight?'

'Oh, goodness me,' said Angela, in sudden terror that this was all a scheme of Barbara's.

'At any other time I might believe it,' said Miss Bell. 'But not now. She knows perfectly well her life is in danger, and she assured me that she would take special care not to get out of the sight of the people who were placed to protect her.'

'We had better go and look for her,' said Angela, exchanging glances with Mr. Hesketh, for it was now more than twenty minutes since she had followed her mysterious quarry to the back door, and whether it were Irina or someone else, the person must surely be some way away by now.

'Yes,' said Hesketh. 'Suppose we split up. Mrs. Marchmont, you and Miss Devlin go across and look in the outbuildings and the summer-house; Miss Bell, you and I shall go around to the front gates. I rather fear she has been lured out under some pretext, and may have been spirited away in a motor-car.'

'Very well,' said Miss Bell. 'Miss Devlin, I believe there are some torches in the Games cupboard. Would you be so good as to fetch them?'

'Certainly,' said Miss Devlin, keen to make amends for what she was rapidly realizing had been an egregious error on her part earlier. She hurried off, and the others began to discuss how best to conduct the search.

'But what about Mr. Everich?' said Miss Bell suddenly. 'I had completely forgotten about him. He must be informed immediately.'

'Is he staying here in the school?' said Angela.

'No,' said Miss Bell. 'He said very generously that since the Princess was evidently under the excellent care of the school and the British Government, there was no need for him to remain on the premises at night, and so he has gone to stay in the village.'

'Well, the British Government can only protect someone who wants to be protected,' said Hesketh, a little tetchily. 'If the silly girl *will* go wandering about at night when she has been specifically instructed to stay indoors, then there's not a lot I can do.'

'If Everich is in the village then we shall be wasting valuable time in fetching him,' said Angela.

'Yes,' said Hesketh. 'The important thing at this moment is to find the Princess, and quickly.'

A thought struck Angela.

'You don't suppose she has gone to meet Everich and he has taken her away to safety, do you?' she said.

'No,' said Hesketh. 'If that were the plan then I am certain Everich would have told me about it. He said only that he was awaiting orders from the Grand Duke's cousin, Count Paul, as to whether Irina ought to be brought back to Morania, and in the meantime he had been charged with the task of helping British Intelligence keep an eye on her.'

Just then, Miss Devlin, still in her dressing-gown and slippers, returned with the torches and the search began. Angela could not blame Mr. Hesketh for not wanting to be paired with the Games mistress, but was rather comforted herself by having Miss Devlin for a partner, having seen the damage that lady could do to a grown man while still half-asleep. They hurried down to the summer-house as instructed and looked in, but saw nobody inside. Angela was beginning to think that they might be too late, for Irina had had ample time to get away if she wished. What on earth had possessed the girl? She knew perfectly well she was in danger. Had she decided to try and return home to Morania by herself? That would be absurd, when she might do it in the company of a member of Moranian Intelligence who had been sent specifically to protect her. Why, then?

'Not here,' said Miss Devlin. 'Let's go and look in the huts over there.'

Without much hope, Angela followed her. They poked about dutifully in each of the outbuildings, but saw nothing.

'It's useless,' said Miss Devlin. 'Why, the child might be anywhere. The school grounds are surrounded by trees and bushes, and it would be as easy as anything for her to hide for as long as she liked.'

'But why?' said Angela.

'Don't ask me,' said Miss Devlin. 'Everyone seems to know much more about the thing than I do. I only wish somebody would tell me what it was all about.'

Angela was just wondering whether she ought to enlighten Miss Devlin on the subject, when the Games mistress stiffened and said:

'Look! Over there!'

Angela turned and thought she saw something dart towards the path along which she had followed Miss Fazackerley the other day.

'Is it Irina?' she said.

'I don't know, but whoever it is they're heading for the village,' said Miss Devlin.

Of one accord, the two women hastened towards the entrance to the path and stopped to listen. Angela thought she could hear something moving in the distance.

'Are you quite certain it was human?' she said.

'I think so,' said Miss Devlin. 'It was someone creeping quite low to the ground, but I'm pretty sure it was a person rather than an animal.'

She did not stop to wait for a reply, but switched on the

torch and ploughed ahead onto the path, Angela following behind. Here under the trees, the moonlight was unable to penetrate and so the torch was a necessary object. They walked briskly along the path, their footsteps making the only sound.

'We ought to go faster,' said Angela, remembering that they were most likely following a young girl who knew she was being pursued. She speeded up her pace, and Miss Devlin followed suit.

They finally emerged on to the road which led to the village and looked in both directions, and there, about a hundred yards away, running towards the village, they saw what looked like the figure of a girl. Even as they watched, a shadow seemed to detach itself from the hedgerow to her left. What happened next was not clear in the dim light, but it seemed to Angela that the shadow stepped out and pulled the girl to the side of the road and out of sight.

'Quick!' exclaimed Angela.

Miss Devlin had seen it too, and the two of them ran as fast as they could towards the spot where the girl had disappeared.

'There,' said Angela.

Miss Devlin shone the torch on the spot at which they thought Irina had disappeared, but they saw nothing. The hedgerow was pristine and undisturbed, and there was no trace of a struggle. For several minutes they scouted about, looking for any sign of the missing girl, but it was no use, and finally they had to give up. They stared at one another in dismay.

'We had better go back and tell Miss Bell and Mr. Hesketh what has happened,' said Angela grimly. 'We are useless by ourselves. Perhaps they will suggest a search-party.'

The two of them returned, defeated, to the school, to find Miss Bell and Mr. Hesketh just returning from their own search. Miss Bell made an unhappy bleating noise when she heard what they had to say.

'Oh dear,' she said. 'What am I going to tell Mr. Everich?'

Hesketh looked as though he were thinking the same thing about Henry Jameson.

'Well, there is nothing you can do at present,' he said. 'I shall call the police now, and later I shall speak to my superiors in London, who will no doubt give me further instructions, but in the meantime I suggest you all go back to bed. It is very late, and two of you are hardly dressed for the cold.'

This last remark was addressed to Miss Bell and Miss Devlin. The two mistresses were with some difficulty persuaded to return indoors—although Miss Bell had no intention of returning to bed, and instead went straight along to her study, there to begin writing a list of things to be done urgently the next day, while Miss Devlin went to her room, rather confused about the events of the night and still wondering secretly why Mr. Hesketh and Mrs. Marchmont had been creeping about together in the dark.

'Hadn't you better go too?' said Hesketh. He was rubbing at his jaw, Angela noticed with some sympathy.

'Are you all right?' she said.

'I think so,' he replied ruefully, 'although of course my pride has taken a dent. I'd like to think that if she hadn't caught me by surprise in the dark I'd have stayed on my feet, at least. Luckily, she doesn't seem to have done too much damage.'

'Good,' said Angela, 'because we need to go back to the village and look for the Princess.'

'What, now?' he said in surprise.

'Yes,' said Angela. 'The man in the barn, don't you remember? I'd forgotten about him in all the excitement tonight, but what if he was the man Miss Devlin and I saw just now? We know where he's staying, and if it *was* he who did it, then he may well have taken Irina back to the barn with him.'

He looked at her for a second and then made up his mind.

'Very well,' he said. 'Do you have your gun?'

'Yes,' she said, showing him.

'Then we had better go. But you must do as I say and keep back if I tell you. To be perfectly frank, Mrs. Marchmont, I'd much prefer to take a man with me for something like this, but failing that, a woman with a gun will have to do.'

'Thank you,' said Angela dryly. 'I shall do my best not to disappoint. But as a matter of fact, there *is* a man we can bring. He's dying for an adventure and he can take us in the car, too, which will be much quicker.'

Little more than five minutes later, the Bentley was speeding back towards the village, with William at the wheel, while Mr. Hesketh sat in the back with Mrs. Marchmont, who had refused to remain behind on the grounds that she alone knew where the barn in question was. Since they did not want to draw attention to their approach, they left the car by the post-office and Angela indicated the lane in which the old barn was situated.

'Now,' said Hesketh quietly. 'Don't forget that the most important thing is to get the Princess back safely. We know that there are people who wish to do her harm, and can only hope that she is still alive. If she is, it is our job to make sure she is returned to the school safe and well. William,' he went on, 'you and I will creep into the barn and apprehend this man, if he is there. Once we have him, Mrs. Marchmont, you shall take care of the Princess.'

Angela and William nodded in understanding, and then they all set off quietly up the lane. Outside the barn they stopped to listen, and then Hesketh and William crept inside. All was silent, and it seemed most unlikely that a mysterious abductor would be able to hold a frightened schoolgirl captive in the building without attracting attention, at the very least. Of course, that was always assuming Irina was still alive, thought Hesketh grimly.

Suddenly, a noise came from the darkest corner of the barn, making the two men jump. It sounded like a foot scraping against the hard floor. Hesketh immediately switched on his torch and shone it towards the sound, hoping to blind whoever it was temporarily and catch him by surprise.

'I know you're in here,' he said. 'Come out, and no funny business.'

'What do you want?' came a whining voice from the corner.

Hesketh and William approached warily and saw, sitting on a heap of blankets, a man. He was dirty and unshaven, and looked as though he had just woken up.

'You know what we want,' said Hesketh. 'We're looking for the Princess. What have you done with her?'

'What are you talking about?' said the man. 'What princess? Is this a joke?'

'It's no joke,' said Hesketh. 'Where is she?'

'I don't know what you're talking about,' said the man again. He noticed the gun that Hesketh was pointing at him and shrank back into his corner. 'Don't shoot me!' he cried. 'I only came in here to sleep. I'm an honest man.'

'Oh yes?' said Hesketh. 'If you're an honest man, then

where did you get these blankets? They don't belong to you, do they?'

'Someone gave them to me,' said the man sulkily.

William, meanwhile, was searching the barn.

'There's nothing here,' he said.

'No, I didn't think so,' said Hesketh. 'Still, we can't let this fellow go just yet. I shouldn't be surprised if he knows something.'

'But I don't, I tell you,' said the man obstinately. 'I came here to see someone. I've been down on my luck and this seemed like a handy place to sleep for a few nights, so that's what I've been doing. I haven't seen any princesses —or any queens or emperors, for that matter, so you might as well save your breath and stop asking me about them.'

Hesketh and William glanced at each other. He seemed sincere enough.

'Get up,' said Hesketh.

'Where are you taking me?' said the man fearfully.

'Up to the school,' said Hesketh. 'I still have some questions to ask you. If you're telling the truth then you'll get a bed, a wash and a hot meal for your pains. If not— well, the Princess had better be safe and well, or it will be the worse for you.'

They bundled the man out of the barn. Angela was waiting for them outside.

'Is this the man you saw?' said Hesketh.

'Yes,' said Angela. 'I take it Irina wasn't there.'

Hesketh shook his head.

'We'll take this fellow back to the school anyway, just in case,' he said.

'You're wasting your time,' said the man.

'What's your name?' said Hesketh.

'Fazackerley, if you must know,' said the man.

'You're related to Miss Fazackerley,' said Angela. 'I saw you together.'

'She's my sister,' he agreed.

'Has she been bringing you food?'

He nodded.

'As I said, I've been down on my luck lately. Joyce disapproves of me but she isn't a bad old stick and won't let me starve.'

That seemed to explain the scene Angela had witnessed between the two the other day. It was looking increasingly as though this man had nothing to do with Irina's disappearance. Still, they could not let him go yet.

They arrived back at the school, and Fazackerley made no protest as they escorted him up to Mr. Hesketh's room and locked him in, perhaps enticed by the comfortable bed and the hot meal he had been promised.

'What are you going to do now?' said Angela to Mr. Hesketh. 'You have nowhere to sleep.'

'It's half past four,' said Hesketh. 'Nearly morning—and I couldn't sleep now even if I wanted to. No, I had better get to work. There will be plenty to do tomorrow—not least explaining to Jameson how I managed to lose the very person I was meant to be protecting. I am going to call the police now, as we will need them for the search.'

'I should like to help if I can,' said Angela. 'I feel rather bad myself that I lost sight of Irina. I ought to have run after her instead of coming back to fetch you, but I had no idea that she was the person I'd been following. I thought it was an intruder.'

'There are many things we might have done different-ly,' said Hesketh, 'but it's no use worrying about it now. The important thing is to get her back, and we can't do much about that until daylight.'

'Then if you don't mind I shall go to bed,' said Angela.

'William, you had better do the same. We may need you tomorrow.'

William went off back to the coach-house, while Hesketh went to look for Miss Bell and ask her to call the police. Angela retired to her room and got back into bed, expecting to lie wide awake until morning. Instead, she fell asleep within minutes.

Chapter Twelve

By HALF PAST eight on Sunday morning Miss Bell, Mr. Hesketh, Mr. Everich and Mrs. Marchmont were all gathered together in Miss Bell's study to discuss how best to proceed following the shocking disappearance of Princess Irina. They were joined by Miss Finch, wary and suspicious, whose bedroom was in another part of the building, which had caused her to miss all the excitement of the previous night. Miss Finch was most put out at not having been informed earlier of Mr. Hesketh's real identity, and her very expression said that she had no intention of believing a word she was told this morning without receiving some proof of it. She was particularly suspicious of Angela, the purpose of whose presence at the meeting was unclear to her, and she darted frequent sideways glances at her.

'Then Miss Devlin was quite happy to do chapel duty this morning?' said Miss Bell, addressing Miss Finch.

'Yes,' said Miss Finch, 'although I'm not quite sure what's got into her. She was muttering something about praying for forgiveness and went quite pink when I asked her what she was talking about.'

Angela here resisted the urge to look across at Mr. Hesketh, whose jaw sported the beginnings of a bruise.

'Good,' said Miss Bell. 'After church I will speak to the rest of the teachers. This is a most terrible situation, and is likely to do untold damage to the school if we cannot resolve it quickly. I am confident that when the teachers are informed of what has occurred, they will do everything in their power to assist. Mr. Everich,' she went on, turning to that gentleman, 'please do not suppose that my only concern is the reputation of Wakeley Court school. Of course, the most vital thing at present is to find Her Highness at once and bring her back safely. I shall not waste time in useless apologies, but please be assured that we are doing our utmost to recover her. Mr. Hesketh has reported her disappearance to the police, who have already begun a search of the area, and today I intend to speak personally to Irina's closest friends, in order to find out whether they can shed any light on the question of why she should have decided to run away.'

'Do the police know who she is?' inquired Everich.

'No,' said Miss Bell. 'We judged it expedient to tell them only that a girl has gone missing and that we are afraid she may have been taken away by an unknown person or persons.'

'Good,' said Everich. 'I think that is best. As you say, this is a very serious matter, and I cannot deny that I am very dismayed that it should have happened. Also, it is most mysterious. Why did she leave the school? Can we be certain that she did it of her own accord?'

'Oh, yes,' said Miss Bell. 'There is no doubt of it. We discovered her disappearance very quickly, and Miss

Devlin and Mrs. Marchmont even chased after her, but she was quite determined not to be caught.'

Everich acknowledged Angela's efforts with a bow in her direction.

'If you have no objection, Madam,' he said to Miss Bell, 'I should also like to speak to Her Highness's friends today and find out what they have to say.'

'Why, certainly,' said Miss Bell. 'There is a small group of girls with whom she is friendly: Barbara Wells, Violet Smedley, Florrie Evans, and one or two others. You shall speak to them all if you like.'

'Barbara Wells, Violet Smedley, Florrie Evans,' repeated Everich, and for some reason he seemed almost relieved at the prospect. 'Ah, yes. I should be very grateful if you could arrange it.'

Angela looked at him curiously. The smooth demeanour of yesterday had quite vanished, and he wore a nervous air—not surprising given the disappearance of his important charge. If Mr. Hesketh was worried about the carpeting he would receive from Henry Jameson when he returned to London, how much worse must it be for Everich? Angela had no idea how they did things in Morania, but she suspected that Everich might lose more than his job if it should turn out that the Princess had come to harm. He was perspiring slightly and rubbing his hands together restlessly. Angela noticed that one of them was bandaged, but could not remember whether it had been like that when she had met him the day before.

Just then, there was a soft knock at the door. Angela, who was nearest, opened it and saw William standing there.

'What is it, William?' she said.

'Pardon the interruption, ma'am,' he said quietly, 'but I

thought you ought to know that Edwards the gardener has gone missing.'

Angela stared at him for a second.

'You'd better come in,' she said.

William entered.

'This is my chauffeur, William,' said Angela to the others. 'He knows about the Princess and helped us in our search last night. When we came to Wakeley Court I gave him the task of keeping an eye on one of the gardeners, who it seems has now disappeared.'

'Do you mean Edwards?' said Hesketh.

'Yes, sir,' said William. 'I heard the servants talking about it. They went to look for him this morning but found that his bed hadn't been slept in and that he'd taken all his things.'

Miss Bell looked surprised.

'Why, you don't think he had anything to do with Irina's disappearance, do you?' she said.

'I don't know, ma'am,' replied William, 'but I thought you would want to know as soon as possible.'

'I don't suppose he told anybody he was going?' said Hesketh.

William shook his head.

'None of the servants I spoke to knew anything about it,' he said.

'We must find out whether anybody knows where he has gone,' said Hesketh. He turned to Miss Bell. 'What exactly do we know about this man Edwards?' he said. 'He is new, I know, and you said he had excellent references, but other than that what can you tell me about him?'

'Well, er—' began Miss Bell, who was used to being in charge and was slightly taken aback at Mr. Hesketh's newly authoritative tone. 'I know he was formerly employed by the Marquess of Bessington, who sang his praises most highly.'

'Oh, then you followed up the references,' said Hesketh.

'Of course I did,' said Miss Bell indignantly. 'I always do. I wrote to the address given and received a letter in reply which assured me of Mr. Edwards' honesty and capability.'

'I shall take a look at that letter later, if you don't mind,' said Hesketh. 'I rather wonder whether it wasn't a forgery.'

'If it *was* Edwards who lured Irina away from the school, I wonder how he did it?' said Angela. 'I suppose he might have sent her a letter purporting to be from someone she trusted. We must ask the girls whether Irina had received any mysterious communications lately.'

'Excuse me if I am a little slow,' said Miss Finch, who could contain her curiosity no longer, 'but am I correct in thinking, Mrs. Marchmont, that your visit to Wakeley Court has nothing in fact to do with the new Mathematics scholarship? It seems to me that you know an awful lot about what has happened for someone who is meant to be merely visiting.'

'I certainly did come here to make arrangements for the scholarship,' Angela assured her. 'That's true enough. However, Mr. Hesketh's superior in the Intelligence office knew that I was intending to visit, and since I have done a little work for him in the past he asked me to help Mr. Hesketh investigate the threat to Princess Irina while I was here.'

'Really?' said Miss Finch, looking Angela up and down in undisguised surprise. 'I must say, I should never have guessed it. You don't look at all like a detective.'

Angela resisted the urge to ask Miss Finch exactly how

she thought a detective ought to look, and merely said politely:

'No?'

Mr. Hesketh glanced at his watch.

'It is nearly nine o'clock,' he said. 'I shall give this Fazackerley fellow a little more time to sleep off whatever it was he was drinking last night, and then I'll go and question him. Does anybody know when Miss Fazackerley is due back?'

'She usually arrives shortly after lunch,' said Miss Finch.

'His hard-luck story may well be true,' said Hesketh. 'Perhaps he really did come just to beg some food and blankets from his sister, but we can't let him go until we are sure of it. I should say he hasn't the wits to plot anything off his own bat, but someone might have paid him to kidnap the Princess and deliver her to the real ringleader. We simply can't be sure at present, and until we are he will have to stay here. He is locked safely in my room for now and so we have nothing to fear from him.'

'Very well,' said Miss Bell.

'In the meantime I had better telephone Mr. Jameson,' said Hesketh. 'He has asked me to keep him informed of developments. I think he is hoping that we will find the Princess before he has to confess all to the Foreign Secretary and the whole thing blows up into an international incident. After that I shall go and speak to the servants and find out what they know of Edwards' movements. Unless you would prefer to do that, Miss Bell?' he said politely.

'No,' said Miss Bell, in tacit acknowledgment of Mr. Hesketh's present authority in the matter. 'I think you had better do it.'

'Very good,' said Hesketh. 'In that case, perhaps you

would be so good as to look out Edwards' letters of reference?'

'Certainly,' said Miss Bell.

'And perhaps Miss Finch can arrange to allow Mr. Everich to speak to the Princess's friends this morning.'

'Of course,' said Miss Finch.

'I think that is all for the present,' said Hesketh. 'The police are scouring the area and so there is little we can do in that regard. All we can do is wait and see what they come up with.'

Everyone nodded and murmured their agreement, and there was a general movement towards the door as everyone went off to do what had been asked of them. Angela and William were left standing in the passage, the only ones who had been given nothing to do. Angela had no intention of being idle, however. She turned to William and smiled.

'Let's go and do some detecting,' she said.

Chapter Thirteen

'WE DIDN'T HAVE MUCH of an opportunity to look around carefully last night,' said Angela as they walked across the grounds. 'Miss Devlin and I were too preoccupied with finding Irina as quickly as possible, and had no time to scout around for clues, or anything of that sort. As a matter of fact, nobody has had much time to think at all, as we've all been too busy chasing about, but we really ought to try and discover exactly what she did after she came outside.'

'Are you quite sure she left of her own accord?' said William.

'As sure as I can be,' said Angela, 'since I was first on the spot, so to speak. I'm fairly certain it was she who woke me up as she passed my room. I followed her downstairs and discovered that she had run out into the grounds. I then wasted far too much time in fetching Mr. Hesketh, and things got a little confused, and by the time we all came downstairs again it was too late. I do wish I'd followed her when I had the chance,' she said. 'I could kick myself for it. Had I run after her at the time then all this might never have happened. But I thought the person I was following was an intruder and didn't particularly want to get into an altercation. I never dreamt for a second it was actually Irina.'

'You weren't to know, ma'am,' said William.

'I suppose not,' she said. 'And there's no use in crying over spilt milk anyway, so I'll just have to try and put things right if I can. Now, then, since we are pretty certain that Irina came out voluntarily, we must ask ourselves why.'

'To meet someone?' said William.

'I think so,' said Angela. 'Unless she was walking in her sleep, I can't think of a single reason why she should suddenly take it into her head to run out of the school grounds and into the village. So, let us assume that she had arranged to meet someone. Where?'

'The summer-house looks like a pretty good place,' said William.

'Don't you think? As I said, we just peeped in quickly last night, but this time I'd like to take a good look around.'

They arrived at the building in question as she spoke, and stopped. There was not much to it; it was merely a little wooden hut, white-painted with a pitched roof, with inside a few old easy chairs and one or two low tables. The girls came in here in the warmer weather to read or day-dream or do nothing at all, but avoided it in the winter as it was damp and draughty and had a tendency to mould. Angela opened the door and they both stepped inside. There was a musty smell of dry, rotten wood—along with something else. Angela sniffed the air delicately.

'Cigarette smoke,' she said. 'Very faint, but someone has been smoking in here.'

William bent down and picked something up. It was a cigarette-end.

'Are the girls allowed to smoke?' he said.

'I sincerely hope not,' said Angela. 'That's not to say they don't do it, of course. Here, let me see.'

She examined the remains of the cigarette. It was a very slim affair of a type with which she was unfamiliar, but other than that she could deduce nothing from it. She gave it up.

'I don't know what I thought it would tell me,' she said. 'All I know is that it's not one of mine, and whoever smoked it wasn't wearing lipstick. Now, is there anything else?'

They poked about a little more, then Angela spotted a small, dark splash of something on the edge of a low table. She peered at it more closely.

'What is that, do you suppose?' she said.

William came to join her.

'It might be blood, I guess,' he said doubtfully. 'It's hard to tell against the wood.'

'It's quite dry,' said Angela.

She took out her handkerchief, rubbed a corner of it against the stain, and then held it up to the light. There was a brownish smear on the fabric.

'It certainly looks like blood,' she said. 'It might have nothing to do with Irina, of course.'

'Even if it does, there's not much of it,' said William.

'No,' said Angela thoughtfully. 'Certainly not enough to have caused whoever shed it too much damage. I'd like to look around outside, though, just to make certain there's no more.'

They left the summer-house and spent some minutes scouring the surrounding ground for clues, but could find nothing conclusive.

'Do you think the person the Princess came to meet waited in the summer-house for her?' said William at last.

'I shouldn't be a bit surprised,' said Angela. 'It was

rather chilly last night and I shouldn't have fancied standing outside for hours myself.'

'But he wasn't here by the time you arrived.'

'Of course not,' said Angela. 'Now that I come to think about it, we must have been making a tremendous racket. Anyone might have heard us coming a mile off. I think Irina probably met whoever it was, and then they heard or saw us coming and crept out before we got here. I don't know what happened after that, but I imagine they must have split up and hidden in the bushes over there, waiting for us to leave. Miss Devlin and I looked around here and then went over to those huts. That gave Irina the opportunity to escape along the path to the village.'

'But what happened to the person she went to meet?'

'I've no idea. Perhaps he was hiding in the bushes too. It would have been easy enough. After all, there were only the two of us and the grounds are pretty big. He might even have escaped on to the path himself, before Irina did.'

'But why?'

'There you have me,' admitted Angela. She glanced about her one last time and then said, 'Let's go and take another look at the spot where she disappeared.'

They followed the path that led through the trees, looking carefully about them as they did so.

'She'd seen us by this time, and started running,' said Angela. 'When we came out from the woods she was already quite a way ahead of us.'

As they emerged on to the road, they saw a police-car approaching, heading in the direction of the village. Evidently the search had begun. They waited for it to pass, then walked along to the place where the man had stepped out and Irina had seemed to disappear into the hedgerow. Although it was Sunday, there were several people about, and so they had to be circumspect in their search. If

Angela had been hoping to find a clue, however, she was disappointed, for even in daylight there was no sign that the hedge had been disturbed at all.

'I was almost certain this was where she vanished,' she said in perplexity. 'It looked as though she went through the hedge here. I suppose my eyes must have been playing tricks on me. The moon was out, but perhaps it was still too dark to get a true picture of what happened.'

'Where exactly was the moon?' said William.

'Over there, I think. Why?' said Angela.

'Why, then, the hedge must have cast a shadow a little way into the road,' said William. 'Are you sure she didn't just disappear into the shadow and keep going?'

Angela considered this.

'I hadn't thought of that,' she said. 'Yes, she might have. We assumed she had gone through the hedge because the man we saw seemed to step out and pull her into it. But I suppose it's always possible that he just drew her to the side of the road and pulled her along in the shadows. But where did they go after that?'

'Let's go and find out,' said William.

They carried on in the direction of the village for another two hundred yards or so, then came to a halt.

'Oh!' said Angela.

They were standing by a narrow gap in the hedgerow which was easily passable with only a little squeeze.

'Do you think this is it?' said William. He peered through the gap. 'There's just a field on the other side,' he said.

'Well, if they didn't want to be seen it would make sense to get off the road as soon as possible,' said Angela.

'I guess so,' said William. He scrambled through the hedge, then held it aside to allow Angela to step through. There was not exactly a path on the other side, but a few yards of bare earth indicated the direction most feet took when they came through this way. The short-cut passed diagonally across the field to a gate. Angela and William headed towards it. The gate in turn led out onto a little path and through a clump of trees.

'Look!' said Angela suddenly, once they were through the gate. She bent over and picked up another cigarette-end. 'It's the same type as before.'

'Then we're on the right track,' said William.

They carried on doggedly through the wood. Beyond it was a wall with another gate in it, and on the other side of that a road. Although the weather had been dry for several weeks, the ground here under the trees was still soft, and they both saw the tyre tracks by the gate at the same time. William crouched down to examine them.

'They had a car waiting here,' said Angela.

'A big one,' agreed William. He held up another cigarette-end. Angela took it. It was the same type again. Angela leaned over the gate and looked up and down the road. One way led back to the village, and the other towards the coast. Presumably the car had taken the latter route.

'So, then,' she said. 'For some reason, the man brought Irina this way and drove off with her in the car that someone had thoughtfully left here earlier.'

'I guess they came this way so as to avoid going through the village,' said William.

'Yes,' said Angela. 'It seems to be a short-cut. But I don't understand the delay.'

'What delay?'

'Why, the delay in their leaving,' said Angela. She saw his puzzled look and explained. 'I followed Irina to the back entrance of the building, then came back to get Mr. Hesketh, but it was at least twenty minutes before Miss

Devlin and I came out to search the grounds, if not more. If this man was intending to kidnap Irina—or even if she was intending to run off with him for some unknown reason, then why was she, at least, still hanging about the summer-house when we got there? One would have thought that she would have taken good care to get away as quickly as possible rather than skulk around as she did. I don't understand it at all.'

'Do you really think she was kidnapped, ma'am?' said William hesitantly. He seemed to be searching carefully for the right words. 'I know she's kind of young, but—'

He seemed unwilling to finish. Angela came to his rescue.

'You're wondering whether she mightn't have run off with some man,' she said. 'I'll admit the thought had occurred to me, and all I can say is that if she has, then I don't envy the Moranians one bit in having to cover *that* up. Or Miss Bell, for that matter. It's hardly going to do much for the school's reputation, having princesses elope all over the place.'

'Still, better that than kidnapping, surely?' said William. 'At least her life isn't in danger this way.'

'Of course, but we still have to get her back,' said Angela. 'I don't know much about royal families, but I'm fairly sure they're not too keen on having their fifteen-year-old heirs apparent run off with strange men in the middle of the night.'

'Probably not,' said William.

They looked around a little longer, then set off back towards Wakeley Court.

'How cross do you think the Moranians will be, exactly, when they find out what's happened?' said Angela as they arrived back at the school. 'You don't suppose they'd invade, do you? I should give something to see Miss Bell's face if Morania declared war on Great Britain all because she didn't hide her keys properly. How would she take it, do you think?'

'I guess she'd have to give herself a detention,' said William.

He then went to see if he could find out anything more about what had happened to Edwards, while Angela went to look for Mr. Hesketh.

Chapter Fourteen

'IF THEY DID GO OFF in a motor-car, then no doubt they are far away by now,' said Mr. Hesketh. 'I wonder which way they went.'

'We assumed they went eastwards, along the coast,' said Angela. 'There doesn't seem much point in hiding a car outside the village in preparation for a quick and secret escape, only to make a terrible racket by driving through the place after all.'

'I suppose not,' agreed Hesketh. 'You're right—it would make far more sense to drive in the other direction. I had better speak to the police about the tyre tracks you found. Perhaps they will be able to tell what kind of car it was.'

They were sitting in Mr. Hesketh's study, whose window faced the front drive. As Angela looked out she saw a crocodile of girls trooping back after church. To look at them one would never have supposed that anything untoward had occurred. Had they been told of Irina's disappearance?

Angela reached into her pocket and handed Hesketh the cigarette-ends.

'We found these, too,' she said. 'There was practically a trail of them from the summer-house to the place where we found the tracks. I don't recognize the type.'

Hesketh examined them.

'Nor do I,' he said at last. 'I should say they were probably foreign, though.' He thought for a moment. 'So, then, whoever smoked these was presumably waiting in the summer-house for Irina. Does that mean he was the same man who snatched her from the road?'

'I don't know if he snatched her, exactly,' said Angela. 'But yes, I assume it's the same man, unless it was someone else who smokes the same kind of cigarette.'

Hesketh was frowning.

'Let me get things quite clear in my mind,' he said. 'We know Irina came out of the school, went to the summer-house and met this man. A little while later she and he heard you and Miss Devlin coming, crept out of the summer-house and hid—presumably in the bushes—while the two of you scouted about. At some point the man escaped along the path through the trees and waited for Irina on the road into the village. She took the same path, and when she caught up to him he pulled her off the road and out of sight. They then went to the car, which the man had thoughtfully hidden earlier, and drove off to an unknown destination.'

'That's clear enough,' said Angela.

'But it doesn't make sense,' said Hesketh. 'I can see that she might have been lured out to the summer-house, but why did she then follow him? She knew she was in danger.'

'Obviously she trusted him,' said Angela.

'I don't understand it at all,' said Hesketh. 'Here she was safe. Why did she go?'

Angela wondered whether to mention the elopement theory. It seemed rather far-fetched. How could a fifteen-year-old girl, who had been brought up to understand the importance of her position for the future of her nation, and who had moreover presumably led the most sheltered of lives, have fallen in with a man and been persuaded to run off with him? And could that man possibly have been Edwards, the gardener, who by all accounts was a most unprepossessing fellow? It seemed most unlikely. But then what was the explanation in that case?

'Have you looked at Edwards' references?' she said hesitantly.

'Yes,' said Hesketh. 'They seem good enough, and Miss Bell has shown me the letter she received from Bessington House. We put through a telephone-call to them earlier, but the Marquess's secretary, who wrote the letter, was out, and we are waiting for him to call back.'

'It seems rather too much of a coincidence that Edwards should have run off just now,' said Angela. 'He must have had something to do with it, surely. I wonder whether he mightn't have been in league with Miss Fazackerley's brother. Have you spoken to Fazackerley, by the way?'

'Yes. His presence in the area just now is most suspicious, of course, but he is sticking obstinately to his story that he came to find his sister and beg some money and food from her.'

'And do you believe him?' said Angela.

'I have the feeling he is probably telling the truth, but of course I should be a fool if I relied solely on my instincts. No, I'm afraid he will have to stay here at least until Miss Fazackerley returns. She is expected back this afternoon.'

'But what if she is in on it too?'

'Then we shall find it out,' said Hesketh simply, and despite his bland demeanour, Angela had no doubt that he could be ruthless in pursuit of the truth if necessary.

'What about Mr. Everich?' said Angela. 'What is he doing to find Irina?'

'I gather he has been speaking to some of the Princess's friends this morning,' said Hesketh. 'I haven't seen him, though, so I don't know whether he has managed to find anything out.'

'I suppose he has been talking to Barbara and her crowd,' said Angela thoughtfully. 'I wonder if perhaps I oughtn't to speak to Barbara myself, and make her understand that she must tell anything she knows. If they *do* know where Irina went I should hate them to keep quiet about it out of some misplaced sense of honour. Girls can be rather odd like that.'

'Yes, do,' said Hesketh. 'She at least might tell you things that she would be unwilling to confess to Everich.'

Just then, there was a knock at the door. It was Miss Bell, accompanied by Everich himself.

'Ah, Mr. Hesketh, I thought we should find you here,' said Miss Bell. 'Have you heard anything from the police at all?'

'No,' replied Hesketh. 'I was just going to telephone them as a matter of fact, as Mrs. Marchmont has found out which way they went. It appears they have escaped by car, and have most probably headed eastwards along the coast, rather than back towards King's Lynn.'

'Indeed?' said Miss Bell. 'How do you know, Mrs. Marchmont?'

Angela explained about the clues she and William had found, and what they most likely meant.

'I see,' said Miss Bell, frowning. 'But are you quite certain there was only one man?'

'We only saw one, although there might have been another waiting in the car for them,' said Angela.

'I meant outside,' said Miss Bell. 'I don't see how one man could have kidnapped Irina and dragged her all the way to the car without someone hearing them. Of course, a man is stronger than a fifteen-year-old girl, but I should have thought she would have tried to fight him off, at least.'

'It rather looks as though she went willingly,' said Angela.

The headmistress met her gaze and Angela saw a look of understanding and concern pass across her face.

'Then you think it may not have been a kidnapping at all?' she said.

'That is impossible,' said Everich, drawing himself up. 'Her Highness is a Princess from one of the oldest and most illustrious royal families in Europe. Are you suggesting she has run away?'

'There doesn't seem to have been a struggle,' said Angela carefully. 'Of course, that doesn't mean she was not abducted. It may be that she knew her kidnapper and thought she could trust him.'

She saw Miss Bell's look of dismay and pitied her. Whatever the case, things did not look good for Wakeley Court school.

'It is quite absurd to imply that Her Highness had any hand in this affair,' said Everich. 'She knows exactly what is expected of her and would never do anything so outrageous as to leave without telling anyone where she was going—especially now, when her father is so gravely ill and the future of Morania rests perhaps on her shoulders. Why, it is unthinkable! And where should she go? There is nowhere. No,' he went on firmly. 'I see the hand of our enemies behind this. They have taken her, that is certain enough. I hope to God we can get her back before any harm comes to her.'

This was a sobering thought and they all paused to digest it for a moment. If Irina really had been abducted by those who wished her country ill, then there was no saying whether or not she was still alive. Angela remembered the blood she had found in the summer-house and tried to take comfort from the fact that there had been so little of it, but she could not forget that she was here because of a supposed assassination plot. If Irina *had* been abducted, then presumably her kidnappers had intended to kill her. If she had not, then she must still be found and brought back. Whatever the case, there was no denying that they had all failed miserably in their task of protecting her.

Chapter Fifteen

'Since Irina has now been missing for nearly twelve hours, I think we have no choice but to let her people know what has happened,' said Miss Bell. 'Mr. Everich, have you had word today of the Grand Duke's condition?'

'I believe there has been no change, madam,' said Everich. 'He is receiving the best possible care, of course, so we can but hope there will be some improvement soon.'

'Then I had better telegraph Count Paul,' said Miss Bell.

'Yes, I think you had better,' said Everich. 'His Excellency has taken over the duties of state from the Grand Duke for the present, and since he is now in charge, he will need to know of this latest terrible development. I have no doubt that he will be very upset to hear what has happened. Quite apart from the implications for Morania itself, the Count is very fond of his cousin, the Princess. I should not be surprised if he were to leave everything in the hands of his ministers and come to England at once himself.'

'Perhaps that would be best,' said Miss Bell. 'How

quickly do you suppose he can get here? Mr. Hesketh, do you happen to have a Continental Bradshaw?'

'The fastest train from Vorgorod takes about forty hours,' said Everich, before Mr. Hesketh could reply.

'Then the very earliest we can expect him is Tuesday morning,' said Miss Bell. 'Very well, I shall go and send the telegram at once, so as to waste no further time.'

She went off before anyone could raise any objections.

'I understand you have been speaking to the Princess's friends this morning,' said Mr. Hesketh to Mr. Everich.

'Yes,' said Everich. 'I have spoken to some of the young ladies, although not all of them.'

'And did they tell you anything?'

Everich shook his head.

'They are very shocked at Her Highness's disappearance, naturally,' he said, 'but they are all quite certain that they know nothing of where she might have gone. It does not surprise me, for how could they know of a criminal plot of this kind? Still, I was not able to speak to all the young ladies this morning, and so I shall try again later once they are all back at the school. I understand that some of them are taken out by their families on Sundays.'

'That is so,' said Hesketh, 'but they are usually back by dinner-time. Perhaps you can try again later.'

'I shall certainly do that,' said Everich. 'It will not do to omit any possible clue, and I confess I was keen to speak to this Miss Evans, for I understand she is in the same form as Her Highness, and thus may know more than the others about her movements last night.'

'Oh, you wanted to speak to Florrie, did you?' said Hesketh. 'Well, I dare say you'll find her about the place later on.'

The lunch-bell rang, and Angela steeled herself against the school's Sunday offering—which, however, was not as bad as she had feared. There was little conversation at lunch. The teachers had of course heard the news, but would not talk about it before the girls. All except Miss Fazackerley were there, for Miss Bell wanted to speak to them after lunch in view of the exceptional events. Mr. Welland had therefore left his mother and Mr. Penkridge his wife to lonely Sunday dinners, and both had come up to the school to see what Miss Bell had to say on the matter, not without some grumbling on the part of Mr. Welland, who hated any inconvenience to himself and saw no reason why he should put himself out, missing princess or no missing princess.

Angela pushed a little heap of under-cooked carrots around her plate and glanced about, wondering whether any of the teachers had had a hand in the affair. It seemed unlikely that Edwards had acted alone, if he was indeed the man she had seen the night before with Irina. But which of them, if any, was the culprit? Old Mr. Penkridge, whose eyes twinkled with good humour and whose moustache wagged up and down as he ate? Impossible, surely. Miss Finch, casting shrewd and suspicious looks in Angela's direction? Perhaps, although her strict and unbending manner seemed more suited to the squashing of unruly schoolgirls than the overthrow of a monarchy. Mlle. Delacroix? She was certainly an independent spirit, and a woman to follow her own path in life, but was she a criminal? Then there was Mr. Welland, who sat at the end of the table, his nose in the air, quite at ease with himself and his own superiority. Angela had not taken him for a man of great intellect, but of all the teachers she thought he was the most likely to be influenced by the prospect of a benefit to himself—money, presumably, in this case. She could quite well believe that he might have been persuaded to trick Irina into leaving the school in exchange for financial reward. And another thing: he had been to Russia recently. Had he perhaps been approached there? She remembered what Henry Jameson had said about the danger from Russia. It would certainly be in that country's interests to place a spy at the school. Her gaze then fell on Miss Devlin, who had been subdued all morning following her adventure of the night before. A greater picture of embarrassed innocence could not present itself, and yet it could not be denied that the Games mistress had played an important part in allowing Irina to escape, with her well-placed blow to Mr. Hesketh's jaw. She had claimed it was an honest mistake, but was that true? Perhaps she had done it deliberately in order to gain more time.

After lunch, they all gathered in the staff common-room to wait for Miss Bell and Mr. Hesketh, who had not been in the dining-room. Mr. Welland threw himself languidly into a chair and yawned.

'And so I understand our esteemed Latin master is in fact a spy,' he said. 'How simply thrilling. Is he going to come and interrogate us now as to what we were doing last night? I take it we are all suspected of having had a hand in kidnapping this tiresome girl.'

'This tiresome girl, as you call her, may well have been taken by people who intend to hurt her,' said Miss Finch, eyeing him with disfavour. 'I know you object to having your time off interrupted, Mr. Welland, but I should have thought you might find it in your heart to feel a little sympathy at least—if only because if any harm *does* come to her, then the reputation of the school is likely to suffer and you may find yourself without a position.'

'N-hem! The reputation of the school is of quite secondary importance at present,' said the kind-hearted Mr. Penkridge. 'This poor girl, Irina. I hate to think of her having been taken away from her friends. And so soon after her father was grievously injured, too! She must be worried sick about him, and missing him terribly.'

'If she is still alive,' said Mam'selle, in a matter-of-fact voice.

There was a chorus of protest and she shrugged.

'We must accept the possibility that she may have been killed,' she said. 'Those who murder for political motives are ruthless and cannot be reasoned with, and it is useless to pretend otherwise. As Mr. Penkridge says, they have already made an attempt on Irina's father, the Grand Duke. It is nothing to them if they kill a young girl too. Of course, I hope that she is still alive, but I am not so stupid as to deny other possibilities.'

'Oh dear,' bleated Miss Devlin unhappily. 'There's going to be the most enormous scandal, isn't there? And it will be all my fault. It was I who stopped Mr. Hesketh from running after Irina and catching her.'

'She had already run outside by that time,' said Angela. 'If anyone is at fault it is I. I could easily have followed her into the grounds, but I went back to get help instead. It's easy enough to blame ourselves, Miss Devlin, but neither of us was to know what would happen.'

'By the way, a little bird tells me that Miss Fazackerley may know something about all this,' said Mr. Welland. 'Where is she, by the way? Isn't she back yet?'

'She ought to have returned by now,' said Miss Finch, looking at her watch. 'Perhaps she caught the slow train.'

Angela frowned as a wisp of thought darted through her head and disappeared.

'What does Miss Fazackerley know?' said Mam'selle with interest.

'Mr. Hesketh can tell you more about that,' said Mr. Welland. 'As can the man he has locked up in his room.'

Not all had heard this part of the story, and so Angela now explained what had happened.

'Miss Fazackerley never mentioned having a brother,' said Miss Finch. 'It all sounded very suspicious to me when I heard about it this morning. I think he must be lying.'

'Not necessarily,' said Angela. 'I have—er—seen them together, so it's certain that they know one another, at least.'

Just then, Miss Bell arrived, accompanied by Mr. Hesketh.

'Has there been any sign of the young lady?' said Mr. Penkridge immediately.

'No,' said Hesketh. 'I have heard from the police, however. They are at present conducting a search all the way along the coast, but of course there's no saying that the fugitives mightn't have turned inland after a while. There are many country roads in which to get lost. It all depends on where they wanted to go—whether they intended to remain here in Norfolk or perhaps spirit the Princess back to London and take her abroad somewhere.'

'Surely they wouldn't need to take her back to London if they wanted to go abroad,' observed Angela. 'There must be lots of harbours along the North coast here from which they could sail if they wished.'

'Yes, there are,' said Hesketh. 'Most of them are too small to take a boat big enough to cross to Holland or Germany, for example, but there's no saying that the kidnappers didn't have one waiting a little further out to sea. There are lots of little fishing-craft hereabouts, and it would be easy enough to reach a bigger boat that way. The sea is a big enough place to hide anybody.'

He did not say that it was also a good place to dispose of a dead body, but it was evident he was thinking it.

'Then there is no possibility of getting her back,' said Mr. Penkridge in dismay.

'I hope there is,' said Mr. Hesketh. 'The police are doing everything they can. They're a pretty efficient lot here, and they've got every man out searching. Norfolk is a quiet place, so of course any strangers tend to be noticed. If anyone saw or heard the car pass, then you can be sure the police will know about it soon enough.'

'Do they know who did it?' said Miss Finch.

'I am very much afraid it looks as though one of our gardeners was involved in the plot,' said Miss Bell uncomfortably.

'Then you have heard from the Marquess of Bessington's secretary?' said Angela, looking from Miss Bell to Mr. Hesketh.

'Yes,' said Hesketh, 'and it appears that Edwards gained his position at the school under wholly false pretences.'

'I regret to say that I was completely taken in by his references,' said Miss Bell. 'The address he gave me purported to be that of the Marquess's London offices, but in fact it was a false one. Nobody at Bessington House had ever heard of Edwards. I shall be more careful in future, naturally.'

'What, that rough-looking fellow?' said Mr. Welland. 'So he did it, did he? Well, I must say I'm hardly surprised. Why, anybody might have known he was a bad 'un.'

'Thank you, Mr. Welland. I shall bear your expertise in mind when I next employ a gardener,' said Miss Bell with some asperity.

'What about this man you have under lock and key upstairs?' said Mam'selle to Mr. Hesketh. 'Mrs. Marchmont says he is Miss Fazackerley's brother.'

Hesketh was about to reply when the door opened and

the Maths mistress herself walked in, having evidently just arrived. She looked around in surprise at the assembled teachers—an unusual sight for a Sunday afternoon—and said:

'Hallo, what's happening here?'

Mr. Hesketh would have preferred to speak to her in private, but he was given no chance to do so, for Miss Finch immediately spoke up.

'Irina Ivanoveti has disappeared,' she said.

'Who?' said Miss Fazackerley.

'The Princess,' said Mam'selle. 'She has been taken away, perhaps by kidnappers.'

'Oh,' said Miss Fazackerley. She saw that something more was expected of her. 'Have the police been called?' she said. 'Who did it?'

'We thought you might be able to answer that,' said Miss Finch before Miss Bell could shoot her a warning look.

'I?' said Miss Fazackerley uncomprehendingly. 'Why, I know nothing about it. I have only just got back, as you see. I have been visiting my mother.'

'What about your brother?' said Mr. Welland, with the merest hint of a sneer. 'Did you visit him too while you were there?'

'My brother?' said Miss Fazackerley. 'What do you know about Dick? Where is he?'

Mr. Hesketh coughed.

'At present he is locked in one of the guest-rooms until we can confirm his story,' he said.

'What story?' said Miss Fazackerley. Finally realization dawned on her, and she gasped. 'You can't mean you think he kidnapped Irina? Why, that's simply nonsense!'

'Are you quite sure of that?' said Miss Bell. 'You must

admit it looks rather odd that he is the only stranger to have been seen in the area lately.'

'Of course I'm sure,' said Miss Fazackerley. 'He came because he knew I was here. He wanted food and a bed. Naturally I couldn't give him a bed, but I did what I could for him and he promised he would leave in a day or two.'

'Are we to understand that he does not have a home of his own?' said Mr. Penkridge kindly.

Miss Fazackerley went pink.

'No, he doesn't,' she said, and looked down. 'He—he was in prison, you see. Not for anything like kidnapping,' she went on hurriedly. 'It's just that he could never settle to anything after the war, and I'm afraid he rather turned to drink. He always had a little weakness that way. He couldn't seem to stay in a job for more than a few weeks, and then one day he was discovered stealing some money from his employer. He would have paid it back, I know he would. He's not a bad person at all, but he wanted something to drink, and the money was there, and—and—' She tailed off unhappily.

'I see,' said Miss Bell, and glanced at Mr. Hesketh.

'Did you say he was here?' said Miss Fazackerley suddenly. 'You haven't hurt him, have you?'

'No, of course not,' said Mr. Hesketh. 'As a matter of fact he has been very well treated.'

'And what do you intend to do with him?' said Miss Fazackerley.

'I think we shall have to hand him over to the police for questioning,' said Mr. Hesketh. Miss Fazackerley was about to protest but he went on, 'I'm sorry, but I have no choice. We can't risk missing any possible clue about Irina's whereabouts. If he knows nothing, then of course they will let him go. Besides, I expect it will do him good to have a warm bed and regular meals for a few days.'

Miss Fazackerley saw that Hesketh's mind was made up.

'Then may I see him, please?' she said.

'Certainly,' said Hesketh. 'In fact, I should be glad of your help, as he is somewhat reluctant to tell me anything. Perhaps he will be more inclined to speak if you are there to encourage him.'

They left the room together, Miss Fazackerley looking slightly dazed. From what Angela had seen, it looked as though the Maths mistress knew nothing of what had happened—the story about her brother was certainly convincing enough—but of course the police and Mr. Hesketh would have to be the judge of that.

'What ought we to do now?' asked Miss Finch of Miss Bell. 'Do the girls know what has happened? Ought we to tell them?'

'Some of them already know,' said Miss Bell, 'which I suppose means they *all* know by now. It certainly cannot be kept a secret for much longer. Still, I suggest we do not say anything about it until the end of the day. Perhaps by that time the police will have found her.'

'I wonder whether she mightn't have run off for a joke,' said Miss Devlin hopefully.

'I should be overjoyed if that were the case,' said Miss Bell. 'However, I fear that this is not a situation which can be easily resolved with lines and detentions. In fact, I am very much afraid that something terrible has happened.'

There was a silence, and all the teachers looked glumly around at each other.

Chapter Sixteen

WHILE THE TEACHERS were talking in the staff common-room, Barbara could be found huddled up in a corner of the Quad under the portico, sheltering from a cold wind that had blown up, with her friends Violet Smedley, Melisande Bartlett-Hendry and Rosabelle Masefield. They had all abandoned any attempt to learn their passage of Virgil for Monday morning's Latin lesson, and instead were talking about the only subject to occupy anybody's mind that day—the disappearance of Princess Irina.

'Do you think that Everich fellow believed us?' said Melisande. 'I told him she never said anything to me about running off.'

'*Did* she say anything to you?' said Barbara.

'Of course not,' said Melisande. 'She didn't really say much to anyone, did she? He seemed to think we were great friends, so I didn't like to tell him differently, but it's not as though she confided in anybody much, is it?'

'No,' said Violet, 'but of course if her life was in danger and she knew about it, then she was bound to be rather wary about whom she trusted, don't you think?'

'I told him she was a very popular girl,' said Rosabelle. They all looked up and she said, 'Well, I thought he'd like to hear that sort of thing. I know it's not exactly true, but if she doesn't come back, I thought it might give some comfort to her people.'

They all looked worried.

'That's rather a horrid thought,' said Barbara. 'I mean to say, I know she wasn't all that much fun, but I should hate to think—' She did not finish the sentence. 'At any rate,' she went on firmly, 'I'm glad we brought her into our set.'

'What did *you* tell Mr. Everich, Barbara?' said Violet.

'Not much,' said Barbara. 'I said he'd be better off speaking to Flo when she gets back. After all, the two of them were—are—in the same form.'

'Florrie's out with her people, I suppose,' said Melisande. 'Isabel ought to be back soon, too, although I don't expect she knows any more than we do.'

'Isn't that Mrs. Marchmont?' said Violet, who had spotted Angela approaching.

'Yes,' said Barbara. 'I'll bet she knows what's happening.'

'Oh, yes, she's a sort of detective, isn't she?' said Rosabelle with interest.

'Go and see what you can find out,' said Melisande.

Barbara needed no further prompting and ran to meet Angela, who had in fact been looking for her god-daughter as she wanted to speak to her. By common consent the two of them headed out towards the lake, where they would be able to talk in private, since nobody else was about, it being too cold to sit out comfortably.

'I gather you know what has happened,' said Angela.

'Oh, yes,' said Barbara. 'That funny-looking man with

the pale hair came out and asked us lots of questions about it this morning. How *did* it happen, exactly?'

Angela gave her a brief summary of the events of the night before, leaving out the part about Miss Devlin and Mr. Hesketh. She also judged it better not to mention Miss Fazackerley's brother. Barbara listened, enthralled.

'I say, you do do some exciting things,' she said. 'How thrilling, to spend the night chasing criminals about the place!'

'I should far rather have stayed in bed, I assure you,' said Angela.

'And so Mr. Hesketh isn't a real Latin master at all!' said Barbara, who seemed to find this the most surprising part of the story. 'I must say, he fooled me rather neatly.'

'He most certainly is a real teacher,' said Angela. 'Don't think this is an excuse to get off Latin.'

'Of course I won't,' said Barbara. She reflected for a moment or two on Angela's story. 'What a pity Irina ran off before you could catch her,' she said, then frowned. 'But Angela, that's not quite what Mr. Everich told us. He said she had been snatched by a man and dragged away by force. He didn't say anything about her running off.'

'That is what I wanted to speak to you about,' said Angela. 'It suited Everich to say that, as of course he is of the belief that Irina was kidnapped. However, that is not exactly my interpretation of things. I saw what happened myself, and the more I think about it the more it seems to me that she disappeared of her own accord.'

'Oh!' said Barbara. 'Do you mean she ran away? But what about the man who took her? You said it was the new gardener. What has he to do with the thing?'

'That's just it—I don't know,' said Angela.

'Don't tell me you think she's eloped with him, because I won't believe you,' said Barbara.

Angela glanced sideways at her god-daughter. So the idea had crossed her mind too.

'You would tell me if you knew of anything of that sort, wouldn't you?' she said carefully. 'This is no time to be protecting your friends out of some silly, misplaced sense of honour.'

'Of course I'd tell you,' said Barbara indignantly. 'What do you take me for? I hope I know what's important. I mean to say, if it was just any ordinary girl I might keep quiet,' (here Angela opened her eyes wide) 'but we can't just have royal princesses running about the country-side with whomever happens to take their fancy, can we? It won't do at all for an heir to the throne. Besides, Wakeley Court is not that sort of place. I mean, I know some of the girls have a tremendous crush on Mr. Welland, but they'd never dream of running off with him. Besides, I'm sure his mother would object.'

'I'm glad to hear it,' said Angela with some emphasis.

'No, I won't believe anybody could possibly want to run away with that man,' went on Barbara. 'Ugh! He was so grubby. And he always had a sneer on his face, as though he knew something you didn't.'

'Did you ever speak to him?' said Angela.

'No, I don't think anyone did,' said Barbara. 'Or at least if they did, then he ignored them.'

Angela wondered why on earth Miss Bell should have wanted to employ such an unprepossessing character in the first place, but could only suppose that she must have been blinded by the name of the Marquess of Bessington.

'I really think she *must* have been kidnapped,' said Barbara. She hesitated. 'I say, Angela,' she went on. 'You don't think she's dead, do you?'

'I hope not,' said Angela soberly.

'I shall feel awfully bad if she is,' said Barbara. 'I only

wish I could have liked her more than I did. But she was frightfully dull, really. Even when I teased her she never seemed to get the joke. She just said "Please?" in that foreign way of hers. To be perfectly truthful, I was only friends with her because I felt sorry for her.'

'That's not a bad thing,' said Angela. 'In fact, it was very kind of you.'

'Do you think so?' said Barbara hopefully. 'I *have* been trying, you know.'

'So Miss Bell tells me,' said Angela with a smile.

They fell silent for a few moments, then a thought struck Barbara.

'I believe you were sent here,' she said suddenly. 'You were, weren't you? I'd just been thinking what a coincidence it was that all this should happen while you were here, but of course it's not a coincidence at all, is it?'

'Well, I *was* asked to keep an eye out for anything suspicious,' admitted Angela.

'And here I was thinking you'd come to see me,' said Barbara. 'A person might be offended at that, you know.'

'I did come to see you,' Angela assured her. 'The question of the Princess came up after Intelligence found out I had connections at the school, but I should certainly have visited anyway.'

'Oh, well,' said Barbara, mollified. 'Were you following them when we saw them in Percham yesterday?'

'No, that was quite accidental,' said Angela.

'I wonder why they left the school when Irina was supposed to be in so much danger,' said Barbara. 'I expect they were plotting together about how to protect her and didn't want to be overheard. But since they sent this fellow over in such a hurry after the attempt on the Grand Duke's life, one would think he'd have managed to do a better job of looking after her, don't you think?'

Angela turned and looked at Barbara thoughtfully, but said nothing. In fact, she had just realized what it was that had been bothering her about Mr. Everich. The attempt on the Grand Duke had been made on Friday morning, and Everich had supposedly been sent to England immediately afterwards to attend to the Princess; how, then, was it that he had arrived at the school on Saturday morning, when the fastest train from Vorgorod took little short of two days, as Everich had told them himself? Why had he lied? What could it mean? For one thing, it certainly meant that he had set off for England at least half a day earlier than he had claimed, for he could not have left Morania any later than Thursday evening if the point about the length of the train journey were true. Of course, it might be that for some unknown reason he had been sent to Wakeley Court *before* the attack on the Grand Duke had taken place, but that was not the story he had told.

Might Everich have had something to do with Irina's disappearance, then? It would have been easy enough for him, of all people, to lure her outside in the middle of the night, since Irina trusted him implicitly. If he had told her that her life was in danger from someone at the school and that she must escape to the summer-house and meet him there, then presumably she would have believed him. He might have instructed her to go to the car with Edwards and wait for him there. That would also explain why she had seemed to be running away: she believed she was escaping from her enemies at school and going with Edwards to a place of safety. Angela suddenly remembered the bandage she had seen on Everich's hand, and the smear of blood she had found in the summer-house. Was there any connection between the two? And if Irina had been there voluntarily then why had blood been shed?

Angela shook her head. Surely Everich had had

nothing to do with the disappearance. If he had, then why was he still here when he presumably had the Princess in his clutches already? Surely he and his accomplice Edwards would have escaped as quickly as possible out of the country before the hue and cry began. Instead, Everich was still here, showing every sign of being worried and upset about the fate of his charge and making inquiries of the Princess's friends. That was not the behaviour one would have expected of him had he already been successful in his mission to kidnap or kill her. But then why had he lied about his journey to England? It made no sense. Angela had the oddest feeling that she was looking at the problem from the wrong angle, and that a vital piece of information was missing. If she could only find that piece of information then all would become clear, she was sure of it. In the meantime, she resolved to mention her suspicions of Everich to Mr. Hesketh as soon as she could.

Chapter Seventeen

FAR AWAY IN VORGOROD, the royal household had been in a great state of confusion ever since Friday morning and the attempt on the life of the Grand Duke Feodor. Naturally, the first thought of everybody had been to carry His Highness to the safety of his own bed as quickly as possible, and then to call in the finest doctors and surgeons in the land. An operation had been performed as a matter of urgency, in the hope of warding off the immediate danger to his life, but the surgeons had emerged shaking their heads with great solemnity, for the Grand Duke had lost a great deal of blood and it was feared that he would not last the night. Still, his customary state of good health was a point in his favour, as was the fact that he had been attended to so quickly, and everybody was now praying fervently that a miracle would occur and His Highness would somehow survive.

Unfortunately, in all the uproar, the would-be assassin had got clean away, and a hunt for him had not begun until some time later. Of course, by that time he had had ample opportunity to make his escape, and there was some doubt as to whether he would ever be found. The sheer audacity of the attempt, which had taken place in the Grand Duke's own private park, had caught everybody quite off guard, and although all those present at the time had been questioned closely about what they had witnessed, nobody had been able to agree on who had done it. Some said they were sure they had seen a man hiding behind a tree shortly before the attack, while others said the shot had come from the top of the boundary wall. Still others said they had seen someone galloping off on horseback immediately afterwards, while one particularly excitable old woman swore that she had seen the devil himself swoop down from the sky and rain bullets upon His Highness. Whatever the case, it looked likely that the hunt would be a difficult one, and it was entirely possible that they would never know for certain who had instigated the attempt, or for what reason.

Friday night passed, and Saturday, and the doctors reported that there had been no significant change in the Grand Duke's condition. He remained mostly unconscious, they said, although he did have occasional short periods of wakefulness in which he did not speak but at least seemed to understand what was said to him, for he had managed to blink his eyes in answer to questions. The doctors shook their heads as they spoke to the assembled well-wishers. They knew a patient's progress in the first few days after an injury of this kind was of the utmost importance. If the Grand Duke did not show signs of a recovery soon, then they feared that even if he survived, he might remain as he was for the rest of his life: a useless invalid who might as well be dead for all the contribution he could make to running the country. For the present, then, Count Paul would remain in charge and all matters of state were to be referred to him.

Given the Grand Duke's apparently tenuous grasp on life, many people would have been very surprised had they been able to witness an exchange which took place on Sunday afternoon in His Highness's bed-chamber. After the assassination attempt the Grand Duke's most trusted doctor, who had attended him for many years and whose loyalty could not be doubted, had announced his intention to assume full authority for His Highness's care whether anybody liked it or not, and had refused absolutely to leave his bedside. Dr. Petek was a fearsome giant of a man, with enormous waving hands and a terrifying manner, and nobody dared contradict him; besides, all knew how the Grand Duke trusted him, for Petek had attended him during a dangerous attack of typhoid fever many years ago and had earned his respect and favour. On that Sunday afternoon, then, one might have expected to see Dr. Petek sitting quietly by His Highness's bedside, watching for any signs of a change in his condition as he lay there, unconscious. Instead, he was attempting to calm a very wide-awake Grand Duke Feodor, who had just learned of his daughter Irina's disappearance and was attempting to get out of bed, despite being swathed in bandages and clearly in no condition to go anywhere.

'Do not be ridiculous,' said Petek, pushing the Grand Duke gently but firmly back against the crisp, white pillows. 'You are in no fit state to get up. I will not allow it. I am only sorry that fellow was stupid enough to talk about it in your presence. I shall have him dismissed from Your Highness's service immediately.'

'You shall do no such thing,' said the Grand Duke. His voice was weak but his eyes were bright and his mind was evidently as sharp as ever. 'You may have authority for my care, Petek, but do not presume to tell me which of my servants I may keep. I am glad he mentioned it, for otherwise it is obvious that you would not have told me of it.'

'Of course I should not have told you of it,' said the doctor. 'Why, shocks of this kind are exactly the sort of thing we must avoid for you at present. You are very ill, and although we have reason to thank God that your condition is much less serious than it might have been, nevertheless it is of vital importance—for the nation as well as for yourself—that Your Highness be given the best of care and not be bothered with bad news.'

'Bothered with bad news!' exclaimed the Grand Duke. 'As though this were a mere matter of a diplomatic snub from the Bulgarians or a disappointing wheat harvest! Why, we are talking about the abduction of my daughter! How could this have happened? She was sent to England specifically in order that she might be out of harm's way, and now I hear that it has all been to no good purpose and they have taken her anyway. I will not be kept in bed at such a time, Petek. Bring me my clothes. I must get up and go to England after her immediately.'

He made another attempt to rise from his bed, but he was after all a very sick man and his outburst had tired him out, and he fell back against the pillows again, panting a little and looking very pale.

'Sire,' said Dr. Petek, regarding him with pity. 'Believe me, if I thought you even nearly well enough to travel, do you suppose for one second that I should prevent you from going after Her Highness? But at present I should not even allow you out into the garden. Here, drink this,' he went on, tipping a few drops from a little bottle into a glass of water. 'It will make you feel better.'

'What is it?' said the Grand Duke. 'I will not be put to sleep.'

'It *is* a sedative, yes,' said the doctor, 'but it will not put you to sleep. It will merely make you a little calmer and more able to think clearly. Of course you wish to direct the search for your daughter, but you cannot do it yourself. I shall not allow it. Drink this and then tell me what you would have me do.'

The Grand Duke winced, for his efforts had caused him no little pain. He saw that Petek was talking sense and took a sip from the glass with reluctance.

'There,' said Petek with satisfaction. 'Now we may think of a plan.'

'Send for Count Paul,' said the Grand Duke. 'I must speak to him.'

'Is that wise?' said the doctor. 'I have been keeping Your Highness's unexpected recovery a secret from the country, you know.'

'What on earth for?' said the Grand Duke in surprise.

'Why, I thought that if everybody believed you to be near death it might induce your assassins to become careless and give themselves away. Since there was evidently a political motive behind the attack, I thought it might be a good idea to watch people and see how they react to your supposed imminent demise.'

'Good gracious, you are a cunning one,' said the Grand Duke, not unimpressed at the doctor's thinking. 'That is clever of you. Still, though, I should like to speak to Paul. He will not give us away. Have him summoned at once.'

A little while later, Count Paul duly presented himself outside the door of the Grand Duke's bed-chamber and was greeted by Dr. Petek.

'Ah, Your Excellency,' said the doctor smoothly.

'How is His Highness?' said Count Paul. His face was drawn and there were lines of worry on his forehead. 'I dare not hope that there has been any improvement?'

'On the contrary, I think you will be pleased to hear that His Highness is now fully conscious and is feeling much better today. Of course, he is still very sick, and there is no question of his being permitted to get up for another week or two at least, but I very much hope that with due care he will make a full recovery.'

Petek took some pleasure in Count Paul's look of surprise.

'Why, that is most excellent news,' said the younger man, 'especially given that the situation looked almost hopeless yesterday.'

'Yes,' said the doctor dryly, and stepped back to allow the Count to pass.

'Paul, my dear boy,' said the Grand Duke as the two men once more entered the bed-chamber.

'But can it be true?' said Count Paul, striding over to his older cousin's bed. 'We all thought that there was no hope, *Velkji Knaz*.'

'Fortunately, it seems that my would-be assassin is not as good a shot as he thought,' said the Grand Duke. 'I am sorry you have been worried, but the good doctor judged it best to let my enemies think they had scored a direct hit. You may go now, Petek.'

'Pardon me, Your Highness, but I cannot think of leaving my charge,' said the doctor. 'However, you may speak as freely as you like. I shall sit over there where I cannot hear you and write out my notes.'

He sat down in a far corner from where he could observe his patient.

'It is useless to argue with him,' said the Grand Duke. 'He will probably stay here forever, and I shall have to give him a knighthood to make him go away.'

'This is no joking matter,' said Count Paul.

The Grand Duke's face darkened.

'No, of course it is not,' he said. 'I have just been informed of Irina's disappearance, and I called you here because I want you to go and find her.'

'Why did they tell you?' said the other. 'You are not well enough to hear such news.'

'She is my daughter, Paul,' said the Grand Duke, and for the first time a look of great anguish crossed his face. 'Please, what do they know of what happened to her?'

Count Paul saw that there was no use in hiding anything from him, and quickly related everything he had heard from Miss Bell and Raul Everich in England.

'And so Everich was there and yet he let her go? How could this happen?' said the Grand Duke.

'I do not know,' said Count Paul. 'He will be disciplined, naturally, but that is not important at present. The vital thing is to find Irina.'

'Is it quite certain that it is Irina who has gone missing, and no-one else?' said the Grand Duke, with a significant glance at the doctor.

'Yes, quite certain, I am afraid,' replied the Count. 'There has been no mistake. Everich was quite clear on the matter.'

'But how could it have happened?' said the Grand Duke. 'We put every precaution in place.'

'I have no idea,' said Count Paul. 'I suspect treachery, but that question will be for another day.'

'Yes,' said the Grand Duke. 'First of all we must find her. Paul, I want you to leave at once for England. Go to the school and leave no stone unturned in your search.'

'I will,' said Count Paul. 'Of course I will. I am sorry it has come to this, *Velkji Knaz*. I thought she would be safe at school. It never occurred to me for an instant that the Krovodanians would go to such lengths to achieve their ends. If only I had known I might have done something to prevent this. I only hope she is safe and well. I cannot bear to think of her coming to harm.'

'You are a good boy, Paul,' said the Grand Duke. 'And you and Irina have always been such good friends—almost like brother and sister. Perhaps this is not the time to confess it, but I always had some idle thought that I should be pleased to see the two of you marry when Irina is old enough. After all, you are not yet thirty, and so are not so much older than she as to make it an unworkable or an unpleasant idea.'

'Really?' said Count Paul in some surprise. 'I had never thought of it myself. I am very fond of her, of course, but I do not suppose she has ever thought of me in that way. Besides, you know it would not be allowed by law. Irina must marry someone of wholly royal blood. My blood is royal only on one side.'

'Yes, it is against the law at present,' agreed the Grand Duke. 'But there is nothing to say the law cannot be changed. If I can give the vote to every man in the country, then surely I can pass a law to allow two people to marry.'

'Can you be serious, sire?' said Count Paul in wonder.

'Very much so,' said the Grand Duke. 'At present I wish for nothing more than to find her, bring her back safely to Morania and protect her for the rest of her life. I shall not be here forever, Paul—as I have been duly reminded these past few days—and it would set my mind at rest to know that Irina has someone to look after her when I am gone.'

'But supposing she does not wish it?'

'Irina is a good girl,' said the Grand Duke. 'If she knows it would make me happy, then she will do it. I should far rather give her to you than to any of these spoilt, effete crown princes one sees so much these days, and I know you will treat her well.'

'I should be honoured, sire,' said Count Paul, drawing himself up.

'Then go and find her,' said the Grand Duke. He clasped the Count's hand and the younger man saw that there was great pain in his eyes. 'Please, Paul, go and find my little Irina and bring her back safely.'

'I will,' said Count Paul.

Chapter Eighteen

ON SUNDAY EVENING at Wakeley Court, Mr. Hesketh was conducting a rather unsatisfactory interview with the local sergeant of police, who had come to make his report.

'Then you have found no trace of them at all?' said Hesketh.

Sergeant Merrow shook his head. He was an alert-looking man with thinning sandy hair and a sharp nose, who had taken with admirable phlegm the revelation of the missing girl's real identity.

'I'm afraid not, sir,' he said. 'Of course, we will keep looking, but we've seen no sign of them at all so far. We have searched all the way along the coast as far as Cromer and beyond—by which I mean to say we have stopped to ask people whether they saw or heard a large motor-car passing some time after three o'clock this morning.'

'And nobody did?'

'Not that they were willing to admit to,' said Merrow. 'We also searched some way inland, but as you probably know, the countryside hereabouts is such a maze of lanes that it would be easy for someone to disappear if they wanted to. Still, we won't give up. We'll keep on searching inland, and tomorrow we'll begin looking beyond Cromer.'

'Have you looked into my suggestion that they might have gone off in a boat?'

'We have, sir, and that is certainly a possibility. As a matter of fact, we did speak to a couple of Swiss holiday-makers just along the road here, at Percham. They are staying in a cottage close to the harbour, and although they can't swear to having heard a car, they did say that they were woken in the night—they can't say exactly at what time—by the sound of a motor-boat putting out to sea.'

'That's interesting,' said Hesketh. 'But can they be sure it was putting out to sea and not coming into shore?'

'I didn't ask them that, to be perfectly truthful,' admitted the sergeant. 'But does it matter? After all, if they escaped by sea then the boat would have to come inland first so they could get into it.'

'True enough,' said Hesketh. 'I wonder if it was our quarry, then. I must get hold of some charts and see where they might have gone. We had thought they might have crossed to Germany.'

'If that's the case then we can't get them back,' said Merrow. 'They might have put in at some other harbour in England, though, and we can certainly inquire as to whether anybody knows anything about that.'

'Do,' said Hesketh. 'And please let me know as soon as you find anything.'

'I shall, sir,' said Merrow.

The sergeant departed and Mr. Hesketh went to Miss Bell's study to make a telephone-call to Henry Jameson. Normally very efficient at his job, Hesketh felt he had rather disgraced himself in this case, and he winced slightly at the memory of Jameson's reaction when he had found out that his subordinate had been flattened by the

Games mistress, of all people. Even now, Hesketh's jaw ached and a splendid bruise was forming, and after a night awake he wanted nothing more than to go to bed with a cold compress and sleep for about twelve hours, but of course that was out of the question with the Princess yet to be found. Besides, Dick Fazackerley was still locked in the guest-room, and Hesketh could not go back to his lodgings in the village either, for he knew his landlady would bombard him with questions about Irina's disappearance.

He made the call and was put through to his superior at home, for Henry Jameson was not one to sit in a draughty office on a Sunday when he might just as well deal with an international crisis in comfort.

'What news?' said Henry.

'Not much, sir,' said Hesketh. 'We've drawn a blank so far. The only possible lead we have is two tourists in Percham who may or may not have heard a boat putting out to sea in the middle of the night. The police are instituting inquiries that way, but if they have escaped to sea then there will be no getting them back. It doesn't look good, I'm afraid.'

Henry sighed.

'Then I suppose I shall have to inform the Foreign Secretary,' he said. 'I know the Moranians have been rather distracted by the shooting of their Grand Duke—which, I imagine, is the only reason they haven't already declared war on us—but sooner or later they will undoubtedly want to know what has happened to their Crown Princess and why we've lost her. It looks as though this is about to blow up into the devil of a diplomatic incident.'

'I'm sorry, sir,' said Hesketh miserably. 'I have failed, I'm afraid.'

'Yes, you have,' said Henry. 'But so have I. I ought to have taken the thing more seriously and sent more people to watch the place. Of course one man and a woman amateur detective couldn't have been expected to keep a princess safe by themselves.'

Hesketh winced at the implied rebuke.

'As a matter of fact, there were three of us,' he said. 'We had Everich too, don't forget.'

'Well, at any rate that will teach me in future never to underestimate a schoolgirl who is determined to do what she wants,' said Henry. 'I have daughters myself and so I ought to have known. Still, it may or may not comfort you to learn that I have had a telegram from Vorgorod to say that they are sending over the Princess's cousin, Count Paul, to assist in the search. I only hope he does not arrive to bad news.'

'So do I, sir,' said Hesketh fervently.

He hung up and went out into the passage, where he saw Angela Marchmont approaching.

'There you are, Mr. Hesketh,' she said. 'I was looking for you and thought you might be here. Where is Miss Bell?'

'Still at dinner, I believe,' he replied.

'Oh, of course,' said Angela. 'I'd forgotten. I'm afraid to say that three days of school meals have been too much for my system, and so when the dinner-bell rang my stomach instructed me in the strongest possible terms to run away and hide in my room.' She saw he was not in the mood to laugh, and went on, 'I take it there has been no further progress in the search. Have you spoken to Henry Jameson? What does he say?'

'I spoke to him just now,' said Hesketh. 'He's not especially pleased.'

'I imagine not,' said Angela. 'I ought to have telephoned him myself, since it was my fault Irina got away. Have the police found any sign of her at all?'

Hesketh told her about the possible clue of the motor-boat.

'It does rather look as though they've got clean away, doesn't it?' she said.

'Yes,' he replied. 'The search has been a failure so far. And we don't even know whether we are searching for a live girl or a dead body.'

They both looked sober.

'If she is dead, then I imagine she will be found soon,' said Angela. 'After all, if the purpose of the kidnapping was assassination, then there is no sense in hiding the evidence. Why, the whole point of it would be to create as great a disturbance as possible.'

'That is true enough,' said Hesketh.

'So, then, as long as she remains undiscovered, there is still hope,' said Angela, 'and we ought to take comfort from that.'

'I only wish I knew exactly what happened last night,' said Hesketh.

'As a matter of fact, that is what I wanted to talk to you about,' said Angela. 'What do you know about Mr. Everich?'

'Everich? Why, he is the head of Moranian Intelligence, sent here to look after the Princess following the attempt on the life of her father.'

'But are you quite sure he is who he says he is?' said Angela.

'Oh, yes,' Hesketh assured her. 'There's no doubt of that. His credentials are quite impeccable. Besides, I have met him once before, a couple of years ago.'

'Yes, and Irina certainly seemed to know him,' said Angela thoughtfully.

'Why do you ask?' said Hesketh.

Angela explained about the train journey and Everich's

apparent lie on the subject, and about the bloodstain in the summer-house.

'I am trying to remember what he told me about his being sent here when Barbara and I met him and Irina in Percham,' she said. 'I don't remember his exact words, but he certainly gave us to understand that he had begun his journey *after* the attempt on the Grand Duke, and that he had been sent here precisely because of the attack.'

'That is what I understood too,' said Hesketh. 'But of course, you are right. If the journey does take forty hours, as he said, then it is not possible that he could have got here by Saturday morning if he left on Friday. He must have been lying about when he set off, then—always supposing he wasn't lying about the length of the train journey.'

'He wasn't,' said Angela. 'I have looked it up in the Bradshaw. He is quite correct.'

'Then I wonder what his game is,' said Hesketh. 'Is he the man we are looking for, do you think? I don't see how he can be—if he is, then why on earth is he still hanging about here?'

'That was exactly my thought,' said Angela. 'If he already has the Princess, then surely he ought to be miles away by now. There's no reason at all for him to stay here. I gather he has spent half the day wandering around the village questioning everybody about whether they've seen her.'

'That's when he wasn't hiding behind pillars here, listening to conversations, presumably,' said Hesketh. 'I hear there have been a few complaints from the girls.'

'I did ask him what he had done to his hand, but he just said he had cut it on a rusty railing in Percham yesterday,' said Angela. 'It might be true, of course. In fact, there's no reason to suppose that the blood in the summer-house means anything at all, let alone that it belongs to Everich. Still, I don't like it, Mr. Hesketh.'

'Nor do I,' said Hesketh, 'but there's nothing we can do about him at present. I'll report your suspicions to Jameson, though. Perhaps he can dig up something about the fellow. In the meantime, we shall just have to keep a wary eye on him.'

Chapter Nineteen

On Monday morning Barbara ran down to breakfast slightly late, having had trouble finding a pair of stockings without holes. She slipped into the dining-room, hoping not to be noticed by Miss Finch, then sat down at her place and looked across at the Fifth Form table.

'You're in luck,' said her neighbour, Rosabelle. 'I don't think anyone saw you.'

'Isn't Florrie down yet?' said Barbara.

'I can't see her,' said Rosabelle. 'She must be late. She'll be in for it. Why?'

'No reason,' said Barbara. 'I just wanted to speak to her, that's all. Did you see her when she came back yesterday?'

'No,' said Rosabelle. 'I haven't seen her for days, as a matter of fact. Didn't she go out with her people?'

'That's what I thought,' said Barbara, 'although she didn't actually say she was going. Did she say anything to you?'

'No,' said Rosabelle. 'Well, she might have, I suppose,

but I probably wasn't listening. You know I never listen to anyone.'

'That's true enough,' said Barbara. 'What about you, Violet? Have you seen her?'

Violet, who was sitting across the table, calmly buttering some toast, shook her head.

'I haven't seen her since late on Saturday,' she said. 'We were sitting out in the Quad for a while, but then I went in because it was getting cold, and I don't know where she went. Did she tell you she was going out?'

'No,' said Barbara. 'But she must have told someone, since we've all been assuming she went out with her people. I say, you don't suppose she's been kidnapped too, do you?'

'Don't be silly,' said Rosabelle. 'More likely she's run away because she couldn't bear any more of this wretched Virgil. Ugh! I shall never remember it. I may have to pretend to faint in the lesson. Don't give me away, will you?'

'If she has been away, then she won't have learnt the Virgil,' said Violet. 'That's probably what she's doing now. I dare say she's in the common-room, cramming like mad.'

But Florrie was not in the common-room. Nor was she in the dorm or the Quad or the San.

'No, I haven't seen her,' said Matron, shooing Barbara away. 'Now, you'd better run, or you'll be late for first lesson.'

Barbara ignored the warning and wandered along to the Fifth Form dormitory, where she found a girl who had run up to fetch a hair-ribbon.

'Hallo, Sarah,' she said. 'I don't suppose you've seen Florrie, have you?'

'No,' said Sarah distractedly. 'Is she back, then? She wasn't here last night.'

She then went off, leaving Barbara deep in thought.

The Latin lesson went rather better than might have been expected—from the girls' point of view at least, since Mr. Hesketh's mind was not on his task, and he absent-mindedly gave full marks to the whole class for the Virgil passage, even though Barbara's pronunciation was execrable and Rosabelle forgot the entire middle section and in desperation conjugated the verb *iacere* instead.

At break-time there was still no sign of Florrie.

'But where can she be?' said Barbara to Violet.

'Why don't we ask someone?' said Violet. 'Look, there's Miss Finch.'

They ran over to speak to the Classics mistress.

'Miss Finch,' began Violet.

'Not now, Violet,' said Miss Finch impatiently. She was looking at something down by the lake. The girls followed her gaze and saw three or four men loading something into one of the rowing-boats.

'Oh,' said Barbara. 'What are they doing?'

Miss Finch said nothing, but set off down to the lake, to ward off any curious inquiries from the girls.

'They're going to drag the lake,' said Violet quietly.

Barbara stared in dismay.

'But that must mean they think Irina is dead,' she said.

'I'm afraid it does,' said Violet.

Just then, Angela came out.

'Angela,' said Barbara. 'They're dragging the lake. They don't really think Irina's dead, do they?'

'Of course they hope she isn't,' said Angela. 'But they must find her, wherever she is, and the lake is as good a place as any to start searching, don't you think?'

The girls stared in horrified fascination as two men climbed into the boat and pushed off from the shore, and another stepped into the shallows and began wading out with a net.

'Do *you* think she's dead, Angela?' said Barbara.

Angela looked at the white faces of the two girls and pitied them.

'I don't know,' she said kindly. 'If she is, then it seems odd that they haven't found her yet.'

'I suppose so,' said Barbara. 'I must say, it was rather silly of her to go wandering about at night. And now Florrie's gone missing too. Or at least, we think she has.'

'Has she? I dare say she'll turn up sooner or later,' said Angela vaguely, and followed Miss Finch down to the lake.

Very little work was done by anyone in the school that afternoon, for everybody was far too fascinated with the search for Princess Irina. No matter how much the teachers scolded, there was no stopping the girls' eyes from turning towards the window and watching the dark shape of the little boat in the distance as it proceeded methodically back and forth across the lake, one man leaning over the stern with the dragging hook.

By five o'clock the light was fading and the men stopped for the day, having found nothing. The girls all watched as the men trooped across the grass towards the school building and were met by Miss Bell, who could be seen pointing to various parts of the grounds, including the woods. Perhaps she was suggesting they begin a search there, too.

Barbara button-holed Violet in the entrance-hall.

'I've just spoken to Miss Devlin,' she said, 'and she says as far as she knows Florrie didn't go out at the weekend.'

'But the Fifth had Games today,' said Violet. 'Didn't Miss Devlin notice she was missing?'

'I don't believe anybody is thinking about anything but Irina,' said Barbara.

'Then we must report it to Miss Finch or Miss Bell,' said Violet firmly.

'But I can't get anyone to listen,' said Barbara.

'Then we must *make* them listen,' said Violet.

They went along to the staff common-room and knocked on the door. Miss Finch answered. Barbara could see all the teachers gathered together in the room behind her. They were evidently discussing that day's events.

'Why aren't you doing your prep?' said Miss Finch. 'Run along, now.'

'But—' said Violet.

'Never mind "but,"' said Miss Finch. 'It will have to wait until later, I'm afraid. We have important things to discuss, and quite frankly I'm surprised at you, Violet. I expected you of all people to have the good sense not to bother the teachers with your childish nonsense at such a time. Now, run along.'

She shut the door.

Violet was quite pink in the face.

'Childish nonsense!' she exclaimed. 'Childish nonsense! Why, I've never been childish in my life!'

'No, I expect you haven't have you?' said Barbara sympathetically. 'Poor you.'

Violet glared at her.

'What do you mean, "poor me?"' she demanded.

'Why, you're always so sensible,' explained Barbara. 'It must be a terrible bore.'

'Oh,' said Violet, and paused. 'But I like being sensible. That's the way I'm made.'

'And very nice you are too,' said Barbara kindly. 'It can't be much fun, though, can it? I mean, always doing what you're told, and sitting prettily with your hands folded, and nodding and smiling and not saying anything when guests come, and always having a clean handkerchief, and being patted on the head and told you're a good girl. Why, I'll bet you've never even climbed a tree.'

'Of course I've never climbed a tree,' said Violet. 'I'd ruin my clothes.'

'Exactly as I thought,' said Barbara. 'And what if you *did* ruin your clothes?'

'Why, I'd get into trouble.'

'But don't you think it would be worth it for the fun you'd had climbing the tree?'

'No,' said Violet.

'Oh,' said Barbara, disconcerted. This possibility had not occurred to her.

There was a brief silence as the two girls contemplated their differences, then:

'Do you really think I'm a bore?' said Violet in a small voice.

'Well, not a bore *exactly*,' said Barbara. 'Perhaps a little staid. Stuck in your ways. That sort of thing.'

'But I've always had to be sensible,' said Violet. 'My family expect so much of me, you see. They're tremendously proud of me. I couldn't let them down.'

'Nobody said you had to let them down,' said Barbara. 'But it's not quite natural to be good *all the time*, don't you think?'

Violet drew herself up. Miss Finch's words had stung her, but she would not suffer being called unnatural and a bore.

'All right, then,' she said. 'Let's go.'

'Where to?' said Barbara.

'To find Florrie, of course,' said Violet.

Chapter Twenty

DESPITE MISS FINCH's apparent dismissal of the matter, the teachers were perfectly well aware that another girl had gone missing, although they had not discovered the fact until that afternoon. Miss Devlin had answered Barbara's inquiry in a hurry, and indeed had had some vague notion herself that they were one short in the hockey, but it was not until the very end of the Games lesson that it finally dawned upon her that she had not seen Florrie Evans all day. On questioning, the rest of the Fifth swore they had not seen her since Saturday night, but all of them had assumed she had gone out with her people, as many of the girls did at weekends. Miss Devlin immediately went up to the Fifth Form dormitory and discovered that Florrie had left all her things behind, including her night-clothes and her purse with a little money in it. This was not conclusive evidence that she had not gone out with her family, of course, but it seemed odd that she should not have taken even a few shillings with her when she went.

On discovering the disappearance, Miss Devlin went white in the face, for she immediately assumed that she would be given the blame for it. She wrung her hands and ran along to Miss Bell's study to announce the bad news and beg forgiveness. Miss Bell took the news in her stride —indeed, there was little that could make the situation worse than it was already—and told Miss Devlin to calm herself.

'Do not worry, Miss Devlin,' she said. 'I shall telephone her people in London at once, and ask whether they have got her. I dare say we shall find out that they *did* take her out, but the fact of it was somehow missed in all the confusion over Irina.'

'But then why hasn't she come back today?' said Miss Devlin. 'Surely they would have let us know.'

'One would have thought so, yes,' said Miss Bell, 'but let us see what they have to say.'

She picked up the receiver and asked to make a call to London.

'There's no reply,' she said after a few minutes. 'I shall try again later.'

They were interrupted just then by Mr. Hesketh and Angela Marchmont. Mr. Hesketh was looking harassed.

'I suppose you have heard nothing,' said Miss Bell.

Hesketh shook his head.

'No,' he said. 'There's still no sign of her.'

'At least we ought to be thankful that they didn't find anything in the lake,' said Miss Bell.

'I have handed Dick Fazackerley over to the police,' said Hesketh. 'They'll keep him for a day or two, but it looks pretty much as though he had nothing to do with it.'

'That is one good thing, then,' said Miss Bell. 'At least I shall not have the worry of being forced to ask Miss Fazackerley to resign. Where do the police intend to search next, Mr. Hesketh?' she went on. 'And is there any point to it? We know where she went, after all—out of the village. I don't know why they thought they'd find her here at the school.'

'They have to be thorough in their search,' replied Hesketh. 'And it's always possible that Mrs. Marchmont and Miss Devlin were mistaken in what they thought they saw.'

'That certainly is a possibility,' said Angela. 'In fact, that's why I'm here. I understand another girl has gone missing, and it's just occurred to me to wonder whether the girl we saw running off wasn't Irina at all, but Florrie Evans. I've been trying to remember what she looked like, but of course it was dark and difficult to see clearly. What do you think, Miss Devlin?'

'You think it might have been Florrie?' said Miss Devlin in surprise. She paused to consider this new idea. 'I certainly thought it was the Princess,' she said after a moment. 'The figure was tall and slim, like Irina, but of course that might have been a trick of the moonlight. Florrie is shorter, but the shadows may have made her look taller.'

'Yes, that's what I thought,' said Angela. 'I assumed it was Irina too, but that's because we didn't know anybody else had gone missing at the time.'

'But that still leaves the question of why,' said Miss Bell. 'Although one might not think it from the appearances of these past few days, we do not encourage our pupils to run off with strange men in the middle of the night. Wakeley Court is not that sort of school.'

She spoke wearily, but with a certain residual pride.

'Was Florrie unhappy at all?' said Angela.

'I don't think so,' said Miss Devlin. 'But of course, girls don't always tell anyone when they're not happy. We do try and look out for signs of it, but if they're determined to keep it to themselves then there's not much we can do about it. She had friends, however, so she can't have been feeling lonely.'

'I wonder whether there was trouble at home,' said Angela. 'That sort of thing might make a girl run away.'

'Still, if the figure you saw on the road *was* Florrie, then that means Irina might be anywhere,' said Mr. Hesketh. 'So it was not exactly a waste of time to drag the lake. Tomorrow I believe the police are going to search the woods, although they will also continue their inquiries along the coast and inland.'

'This whole thing is becoming more and more mysterious,' said Miss Devlin.

'The most important thing is to find the Princess,' said Mr. Hesketh. 'Florrie must wait, I am afraid. I dare say we shall find out that her disappearance is some schoolgirl prank.'

'I only hope you are right,' said Miss Bell.

'By the way, the Foreign Office has been told of what has happened,' said Hesketh. 'They are not especially happy, as you can probably imagine. And I understand that the Princess's cousin, Count Paul, is also travelling here as fast as he can. He is expected tomorrow morning. I have heard *one* piece of good news, however, which is that Irina's father, the Grand Duke, is much less gravely ill than had been initially reported. He is still very unwell, but he is no longer considered to be in danger.'

'That *is* good news,' said the headmistress. 'Then I suppose one ought to be thankful that Morania still has *one* person to fill the throne. All we have to do now is find his daughter.'

Just then the telephone-bell rang. Miss Bell answered it.

'It is the police,' she said. 'They want to speak to you, Mr. Hesketh.'

Hesketh took the receiver. He listened, and the expression on his face changed to one of astonishment.

'Good Lord!' he exclaimed. 'Are you quite sure? But what—why, certainly. Yes, by all means, bring her here. We shall expect you shortly.'

He replaced the receiver and looked around at the three women. The joy and relief on his face was plain to see.

'They've found the Princess,' he said. 'And she's alive!'

Chapter Twenty-One

THERE WAS little to tell about how Princess Irina had been found, for the police had had nothing to do with it. All they could say was that at about half past four that afternoon, a girl had walked into the police station in Percham and claimed to be the missing princess. A very few questions had proved her to be telling the truth, and there was great astonishment and a sudden flurry of activity on the part of the police when they realized what a momentous event had just occurred. They whisked the girl into a private room, gave her the most comfortable chair in the place and called a doctor, who came, examined Irina, peered into her eyes and at last announced that she was in good health, although he suspected she might have been previously drugged. He recommended that she be taken back to the school, given a good night's sleep and questioned in the morning. This, however, was impossible, for it was vital that the police hear the Princess's story immediately, since there were dangerous men at large and they must be caught quickly—and indeed Irina herself seemed willing enough to tell all she knew, although she said she would not speak until she was back at the school, for she would feel much safer if Mr. Everich were there.

The police agreed to this, and within an hour of Mr. Hesketh's being informed of Irina's reappearance, therefore, a police-car could be seen sweeping up the school drive, carrying its precious cargo, while the news swept through the building that Irina Ivanoveti had been found safe and well. She was hurried inside, looking pale and frightened but otherwise in good health, and given something to eat in the headmistress's study. Meanwhile, telegrams were sent and received, and telephone-calls were made, and there was much muted jubilation on the part of all concerned. Of course, there was still the question of where the Princess had been hidden for the past two days, but that could wait. The most important thing was that she had been found alive and well, and everyone from Miss Bell and Mr. Hesketh at Wakeley Court to Henry Jameson and the Foreign Secretary in London could now breathe a sigh of relief at the thought of a diplomatic crisis narrowly averted.

While Irina ate, Mr. Everich, who had been overjoyed at the news of her return, hovered outside Miss Bell's study, demanding repeatedly to speak to her. Mr. Hesketh had no intention of allowing Everich to see Irina alone, having been alerted by Angela to the Moranian Intelligence man's suspicious behaviour, and he merely said that Mr. Everich would have the opportunity to speak to Her Highness later, once she had told the police everything she knew. However, in this he was thwarted by Irina herself, who insisted on her bodyguard's being present during the questioning, and so Hesketh had no choice but to comply.

At last Irina announced that she was ready to tell what

had happened, and so Sergeant Merrow began the gentle questioning while Hesketh, Everich, Angela and Miss Bell looked on and listened. The story she told was an extraordinary one. It appeared that late on Saturday evening, after her return from Percham, she had found a note in her school-bag which purported to be from Mr. Everich. According to the note, Everich had just discovered that one of the teachers had been placed at the school by the enemy, and that Irina's life was in imminent danger if she did not come away with him immediately. He assured her that Count Paul had been informed of the matter and had agreed upon this as the best course of action, since they did not know the exact identity of the spy and thus the safest thing would be to spirit Her Highness away as quickly as possible before the teacher in question could be spurred on to act. The note said that Irina must speak to no-one about it, but must wait until Miss Bell was sound asleep, then take the headmistress's keys, creep outside and meet Everich in the summer-house, whence they would make their escape.

Irina was surprised at the note, especially since she had spent the afternoon in the company of Mr. Everich and he had said nothing of this at the time, but it never once occurred to her that it might be a fake. Accordingly, therefore, she did as she was bid and crept out to the summer-house in the dead of night. When she arrived she found no-one there, but pinned to the door was another note which said that Everich had unfortunately been unable to meet her as planned, and that she should leave the school and go into the village, where she would find him waiting for her by the church.

Irina was just wondering whether or not to do as the note said when she heard voices and saw two people approaching with a torch. She immediately remembered the warning that she was in danger from one of the teachers, and was thrown into a panic, believing that they must be coming after her. The only thing she could think of to do at that moment was to go and hide in the bushes, so she did. She remained there in fear for several minutes while the newcomers searched the summer-house, and when they turned away to focus their attention on the outbuildings she saw her opportunity and ran for it along the path through the woods to the road. She could hear the two people hurrying after her, and this made her even more afraid. She ran as fast as she could until she reached the road, and then set off towards the village and the church, where she expected to meet Mr. Everich.

This part of the story ended here, however, for Irina could remember nothing of what had happened after that. The next thing she knew was that she was lying on a bed in a tiny room, without any idea of how she had got there, and that it was day-time. She tried to sit up but her head was aching, and so she gave it up until she saw that whoever had put her in the room had left her some water. She drank it and after a little while began to feel better. She got up and went to the door but found that it was locked.

'Was there a window?' said Sergeant Merrow.

'Yes,' said Irina. 'It, too, was locked.'

'What could you see from it?'

'Nothing,' said Irina. 'Just a brick wall, and perhaps twenty feet below a little alley.'

'Then you were upstairs. Did you have any idea where you might be?'

'No,' said Irina, shaking her head. 'Only that we were not far from the sea.'

'How do you know?' said Hesketh.

'I could hear the—how do you call them?—seagulls crying,' said Irina.

'I see,' said Merrow. 'What happened after that?'

'I waited for a long time, but nobody came,' said Irina. 'After a while I began to get hungry and I wondered whether the people who had taken me planned to starve me to death. I was frightened, but then I heard the door rattle and a man came in with some food. He did not say anything but just put down the tray and went out before I could ask him why he had kidnapped me.'

'Did you recognize the man?' said Hesketh.

'Not at first,' said Irina. 'But the afternoon was long and I began to think, and eventually I remembered that I knew him, although I did not know his name. He is a gardener here at the school—a great, ugly brute.'

'Did you hear anything from elsewhere in the house?' said Hesketh.

'Yes,' said Irina. 'From time to time I could hear voices of men talking.'

'How many men?'

'Two, I think,' said Irina, glancing over at Everich, who was regarding her with a sympathetic smile.

'Did you hear what they said?'

'No. They were downstairs, and the sound was too muffled,' said Irina. 'Later, when it was getting dark, the same man brought me some more food but would not answer my questions when I spoke to him. I spent the whole of that night awake, wondering what was happening at school and whether I had been missed—and most of all, what was to become of me.'

Here she gave a little shudder.

'You need not answer the questions now if you do not wish it,' said Everich, but she shook her head.

'No,' she said firmly. 'Now I am safe and not frightened any more. I will answer any questions you like.'

'Good girl,' said Mr. Hesketh approvingly. 'Then please go on. What happened the next day?'

'The man came in and brought me breakfast, but he still refused to speak to me,' said the Princess. 'I became a little angry then, and tried to run towards the door, but he blocked my way and pushed me down into a chair, and said in my language that I was not to go anywhere.'

'Then he was Moranian?' said Hesketh.

Irina hesitated.

'I am not sure,' she said. 'He spoke with a strange accent. I think perhaps he might have been Krovodanian, but I cannot be certain of it.'

Here, Everich uttered an exclamation in his own language, then apologized.

'I beg your pardon,' he said. 'This is the very thing from which we were trying to protect Her Highness, and it appears we failed completely.'

Irina again threw him a glance, and went on:

'I sat in the same little room all yesterday, until the middle of the afternoon, I think. Everything was silent and it was very dull, but then suddenly I heard a knock at the door downstairs and the voices started again. I think it was the same two people as before—Edwards and another man. But this time they were not polite for long. I heard them raise their voices and it was obvious that they were arguing about what to do with me, although I could not hear exactly what was said. They shouted at one another for a few minutes, and then I heard a loud noise, like someone falling, and a gasp. Then I heard heavy footsteps, and the sound of the front door opening and closing, and after that there was silence.'

She looked around and seemed not unsatisfied with the effect her story was having on her listeners, who were all agog.

'What happened after that?' said Sergeant Merrow.

'Well, of course I did not know what to do,' said Irina. 'I waited and waited, but I did not hear a thing—not even the sound of footsteps walking about downstairs, and so it seemed to me that perhaps they had gone out. Without thinking I tried the handle of the door to my room, and to my astonishment I found it was unlocked, so I crept downstairs as quietly as I possibly could, opened the front door and ran out into the street. I ran and ran and ran until I could run no more, and then I stopped a woman and asked her please to tell me the way to the police station, and she did, and then I knew I was safe at last.'

'Didn't you see anything of the two men when you came downstairs?' said Merrow.

'Nothing,' said Irina. 'I think the house was empty. I believe they must have changed their minds and decided to let me go. Perhaps they crept upstairs and unlocked the door without my hearing them, and then escaped.'

'That seems rather an odd thing to do, since they'd gone to all the trouble of kidnapping you,' said Hesketh. 'I think it's more likely that your captor simply forgot to lock the door after him. I wonder where the two men went. I don't suppose you saw the second man at all?'

'No,' said Irina. 'I heard only his voice. The only man I saw was Edwards.'

Here Angela frowned but said nothing. Mr. Hesketh and Sergeant Merrow continued questioning Irina for a few more minutes, but it was evident that she knew little more than she had already told. She had obviously been drugged, carried off to a house in Percham, and held prisoner there until her escape, but beyond that they were little further forward in finding out who was responsible— for Edwards had certainly not acted alone—and indeed, from what Irina had said, it did not sound as though he had been the man in charge of things. Perhaps this second man was the ringleader, but who was he? Until they found him they might never know exactly what had happened. All they could do was to keep searching for Edwards. Once he was under arrest he might be induced to speak.

'Well, if that is all, gentlemen, then I think we might allow Irina to go,' said Miss Bell. 'She has been away for two days and I am sure her friends would like to see her and welcome her back before she goes to bed. We are all very glad about your safe return, Irina,' she went on, 'and I know your father will be overjoyed to hear the news, for he has been very worried about you.'

'I, too, am very happy to be back,' said Irina.

'Mr. Hesketh, suppose you take her to Miss Finch,' said the headmistress. 'She will be in need of a good night's sleep after her ordeal. She can stay in my room again. We shall have to keep a close eye on her, at least until Edwards is caught.'

Just as everyone was leaving the room, the telephone-bell rang. It was a call for Sergeant Merrow from the Percham police station and he remained behind to take it. A minute or two later he came out into the corridor to find Mr. Hesketh and Mr. Everich vying with apparent polite-ness over which of them should look after Irina. Neither had the slightest intention of leaving her to the other, and it looked as though an impasse had been reached.

'Might I speak to you for a moment, Mr. Hesketh, sir?' said Merrow.

Hesketh grimaced and glanced at Angela, who fortu-nately was still present and gave him to understand silently that she would keep an eye on the Princess and Everich. Hesketh returned into Miss Bell's study with the sergeant.

'What is it?' he said.

'It looks as though Edwards has been found, sir,' said Sergeant Merrow.

'Arrested?' said Hesketh, although it was perfectly obvious from the sergeant's face what he meant.

'No, sir,' said Merrow. 'Dead on the beach with his throat cut. He won't be able to tell us anything now.'

'Damn,' said Mr. Hesketh. He sighed and rubbed his face tiredly. 'I take it this other fellow did it. If what the girl says is true, then it looks as though there was a disagreement between them as to what to do with her. Funny, since I thought the whole point of taking her in the first place was to kill her.'

'Not a pleasant thought, sir, is it?' said Sergeant Merrow. 'I mean, killing a little girl for political reasons. I don't excuse murder, but I can understand why people do it when they have a personal grudge against someone. To kill a person you've never met and don't care a fig for, though—why, that's a different thing altogether. It's just plain wicked.'

'That's true enough,' said Hesketh. 'I don't suppose your men have any witnesses to Edwards' murder?'

'No. They're still searching the area for clues, although the darkness is going to make it difficult, of course. Apparently the body was found an hour or two ago by a man walking his dogs, who came and reported it to them in a great hurry. Of course they went to the beach immediately and identified it quickly as that of Edwards, since they already had a description of him.'

'You said his throat was cut. That sort of thing leaves a lot of blood. Do they know if he was killed where he was found?'

'Difficult to say, sir,' said the sergeant. 'His body was left at the high tide mark and the waves were lapping over him when the man found him, so any blood would have been washed away.'

'Hmm,' said Hesketh. 'I wonder whether that was deliberate, or whether the murderer just happened to pick that spot by chance.'

'Didn't the young lady mention having heard the sounds of a struggle?' said Merrow suddenly. 'I wonder whether the murder mightn't have happened then.'

'It's possible,' said Hesketh. 'Although how the murderer managed to carry a dead body covered in blood all the way to the beach in the middle of the afternoon without being spotted is beyond me. You shall have to put your men on to finding that house, Merrow. It ought to be easy enough from Irina's description. After all, Percham is a small place, and someone must have noticed *something* going on.'

'I've no doubt we'll find it soon enough,' said Merrow. 'And once we do, I dare say that will lead us to the identity of the second man. Now, if you'll excuse me, sir, I'm wanted back in Percham. I shall let you know as soon as we discover anything.'

He departed, leaving Hesketh to inform the proper people of what had happened to Edwards. Miss Bell exclaimed in dismay at the news, although in reality she was half-relieved, for that seemed to dispose of at least part of the problem very neatly. One of Irina's kidnappers was dead, and she had no doubt that the other one would be caught very soon. The Princess was back where she belonged, and Wakeley Court was once more a place to which one's daughters might be safely sent without fear of their being rudely abducted by foreign assassins. Most importantly, there was every chance that the story might be hushed up before a scandal developed, and the reputation of the school preserved. The headmistress breathed a little sigh of relief and thought of Irina, sleeping peacefully upstairs. She had been locked in from the outside this time—although the very idea of her running off again was absurd—and when Miss Bell went up later on she found the girl lying fast asleep as though nothing had happened. She gazed at Irina for a moment, and quite possibly offered up a silent prayer of thanks, then got into bed and put her keys under the pillow.

Chapter Twenty-Two

MEANWHILE, the hunt for Florrie Evans had begun. Since it was not yet dinner-time, Violet proposed their going to speak to the girls in the Fifth Form common-room.

'Oh, it's you again, is it?' said Sarah, eyeing Barbara with impatience. 'No, we don't know where Florrie has gone, and no, there's no use in your asking us about it again. We couldn't tell Miss Devlin anything and we can't tell you anything either. Now, you'd better buzz off, as we've got the most awful Geography test tomorrow and we haven't got time for anything else.'

'Oh, Miss Devlin knows, does she?' said Violet, but Sarah made shooing motions with her hands and they had no choice but to leave.

'Let's go and look through her things,' said Barbara. 'We might find a clue there.'

They went up to the Fifth Form dorm, which strictly speaking was supposed to be out of bounds, and began snooping through the little chest of drawers that was next to Florrie's bed.

'I only wish we knew what we were looking for,' said

Barbara. 'I suppose it's too much to hope for that we'll find a letter scrawled in blood that says, "Help! I have been taken by White Slavers and am being held prisoner in the old granary near Burnham Market."'

'You don't *really* hope for that, do you?' said Violet, who was not yet fully accustomed to Barbara's odd sense of humour.

'Of course not, silly,' said Barbara. 'I was just using it as an example. There's no such letter, anyway.'

'There are no letters at all, in fact,' said Violet. 'Don't you think that's rather odd?'

'Why?'

'Well, don't you get letters?'

'Of course I do,' said Barbara.

'And so do I. But Florrie doesn't seem to have any.'

'Perhaps her people never write to her,' said Barbara.

'That's rather sad, don't you think?' said Violet. She frowned. 'And it's just occurred to me: what exactly *do* we know about her family? Has she ever told you anything about them?'

'No, now that you mention it, I don't believe she has,' said Barbara. 'Perhaps she's an orphan.'

'You're an orphan too, aren't you? But you get plenty of letters,' said Violet.

'That's true enough,' agreed Barbara. 'Yes, I see what you mean. It is rather strange. I wonder why she's never said anything about her people.'

'And if she doesn't get letters, then presumably nobody comes to take her out on Saturdays and Sundays either,' said Violet, who liked to pursue a train of thought to the end.

'Do you think she has run away, then?' said Barbara. 'I say, I hope it's not because of anything I've done. I should hate to think I'd made her unhappy.'

'I don't believe it's anything like that,' said Violet. 'She didn't seem unhappy to me at all. Oh!' she exclaimed, as she suddenly remembered something. 'She did get a letter, though. Of course she did.' Barbara looked at her questioningly, and she continued, 'It was on Saturday. We went out to sit in the Quad and she had a letter then. I remember she was reading it.'

'Who was it from?' said Barbara.

'I don't know,' said Violet. 'She was holding it so I couldn't see. Besides,' she went on primly, 'you don't suppose I read other people's letters over their shoulders, do you?'

'No, but there's no reason why she shouldn't have told you who sent it,' said Barbara. 'I mean to say, it's the sort of thing one would mention, isn't it?'

'Well, the letter isn't here, at any rate,' said Violet. 'She must have taken it with her when she left.'

'She didn't take any money, though,' said Barbara. 'I don't understand it at all. Why would she take a letter but no money?'

'How do you know she didn't take any money?'

'Because the other day she told me she'd spent all last week's, and when we went to get some more Matron gave her this ten-shilling note. Look, you can see someone's been doing sums on it. That's how I remember. There's just this and a few pennies in her purse, so she can't have taken any with her.'

'If this was all the money she had, then she can't have gone too far,' said Violet, thinking. 'I mean, she can't have taken the train home or anything like that.'

'Then she must be somewhere around here,' said Barbara. 'Do you suppose she's gone to hide in the village?'

'But where?' said Violet.

Barbara had no chance to reply, for just then they were

discovered by a Fifth Former, who roundly chastised them, firstly for being present in the Fifth Form dorm at all, and secondly for snooping through another girl's things, and threatened to report them to Miss Finch.

'But we're looking for Florrie,' protested Barbara. 'We thought there might be a clue here.'

'Out!' said the girl, and they were forced to leave before she carried out her threat.

At dinner they put their heads together as they tried to think of where Florrie might have gone.

'Do you think she ran away because of this letter, then?' said Barbara.

'I can't think of any other reason,' said Violet.

Barbara gasped suddenly as an idea struck her.

'She must have been kidnapped!' she said.

'Don't be absurd,' said Violet. 'Who would want to kidnap Florrie?'

'Why, the same people who took Irina, of course,' said Barbara. 'That must be it, I'm sure of it. Why else would she have gone missing at the same time? It's far too much of a coincidence.'

'But why did they take her?' said Violet.

Barbara was thinking.

'Perhaps Florrie and Irina went out together on Saturday night. I expect Irina was frightened of the dark, or something, and insisted on having company. That's what Florrie's letter was—a note from Irina asking her to come out with her in the middle of the night. They were both taken together, I'm certain of it!'

'Are you sure?' said Violet doubtfully. 'I suppose it's possible.'

'Of course it's possible,' said Barbara. 'It's the only explanation that makes sense. Why, it's ridiculous to imagine that both of them went missing separately on the very same day. They must have gone together.'

It seemed rather far-fetched, but Violet was forced to admit that Barbara might have a point.

'But in that case, if they did go together, there's no sense in our continuing to search around here,' she said. 'They've most probably been taken far away and the police have all that in hand.'

'Yes, I suppose they do,' said Barbara soberly, as she remembered the dragging of the lake that afternoon. 'Very well, then, let's give it up for now. Do you think there's any use in our telling Miss Bell what we think happened?'

'I doubt it. They won't want to hear any *childish* theories from us, will they?' said Violet with some bitterness.

'Still, though, I think we ought to,' said Barbara, who was used to being reprimanded and was thus less affected by what adults thought of her.

'You do it, then,' said Violet.

As it happened, there was no need for either of them to do it, for shortly after dinner the news came that Princess Irina had been found alive and safe. No details were given, but no mention was made of Florrie Evans either, and when Barbara asked Miss Devlin whether Florrie had been found too the Games mistress shook her head but was too distracted to answer any further questions. It looked, therefore, as though they were back where they started.

'All right, then,' said Barbara, as she and Violet huddled together in a corner of the common-room. 'Let's try and think about it from Florrie's point of view. I still say there's a connection between her disappearance and Irina's, but none of the teachers are likely to tell *us* what they know so we'll have to think it out for ourselves. Let's start by assuming that Florrie went out with Irina on Saturday night and was kidnapped with her.'

'She wasn't, though, was she?' said Violet suddenly. 'Don't you remember? Mr. Everich told us that Irina was seen running into the village, but he never said anything about a second girl.'

'Oh, yes,' said Barbara. 'I'd forgotten about that. Well, then, let's suppose that she went out with Irina but somehow escaped in all the confusion. Where did she go?'

'If it happened as you say, then she *ought* to have run back to the school and asked Miss Bell to call the police,' said Violet.

'She didn't, though,' said Barbara. 'I wonder why not.'

'Perhaps she couldn't,' said Violet.

'But why?' said Barbara. 'Do you mean she broke her ankle and couldn't move, or something?'

'Hardly,' said Violet. 'They'd have found her by now if that were the case. No, I was thinking more on the lines of her running off to hide somewhere.'

'But still, she'd have come out by now, wouldn't she?' said Barbara.

This was a facer, Violet had to admit.

'Perhaps she was frightened of something,' she said at last.

'What, though?'

'I don't know,' said Violet.

The two girls stared at one another with worried expressions.

'I'm awfully afraid something's happened to her,' said Barbara.

'Then let's stop talking about it and go and look for her,' said Violet with sudden decision. 'We can't go chasing across the country after her, but at the very least we can search around here. The grounds are big enough, after all. She might be anywhere.'

'Well, she's not in the lake, at any rate,' said Barbara.

'Look here, it's too dark to go out now, but we might scout around inside for a bit. It's always possible that she's hiding somewhere in the building.'

'All right. Where shall we look first?'

'Well, there's no use in searching any of the downstairs rooms, is there?' said Barbara. 'They're all in use. And the servants are in and out of their quarters all day long, so there'd be nowhere to hide in that part of the building.'

'What about a cupboard?' said Violet. 'A cupboard would make a good hiding-place.'

'Not for three days,' said Barbara. 'No, if she's anywhere indoors she'll be upstairs, probably in the attics. Let's go and look there, shall we? No—first we'll need a torch. I'll run up and get one, and meet you by the door to the attic stairs.'

'Where is it?' said Violet. 'I've never been. And I thought the attics were out of bounds to us girls. Didn't you promise that you wouldn't go up again?'

Barbara regarded her pityingly.

'Yes, I did,' she said, 'but this is important. Look here, you do know that we'll have to break a rule or two if we're going to find Florrie, don't you?'

'Ye-es,' said Violet doubtfully.

'Well, come on, then,' said Barbara.

Five minutes later they were standing at the foot of the stairs to the third floor corridor, which, as Violet had pointed out, the girls were forbidden to enter. It was home to the kitchen-maids and the cook, and at present was likely to be quite deserted since the servants would all still be clearing up after dinner.

'It's up here,' said Barbara and put a foot on the bottom stair. No sooner had she done so than they heard a sharp voice addressing them and they jumped. It was Miss Finch, who had just come out of a room to their left.

'Girls!' she said. 'What do you think you're doing? You know perfectly well that you are not allowed to enter this part of the building. Violet, I am surprised at you. I'm afraid this will mean a black mark for you both.'

Violet went a deep pink but held her tongue as Miss Finch escorted the two of them back downstairs, scolding all the while, then gave them some lines and forbade them from leaving the Fourth Form common-room for the rest of the evening.

'But what were you doing going up to the attics anyway?' said Melisande Bartlett-Hendry in surprise, when she heard what had happened. 'It'll be pitch dark up there, and you know it's haunted.'

'Of course it's not haunted,' said Barbara. 'I told you, that was me banging about.'

'What, all yesterday?' said Melisande.

'Don't be silly,' said Barbara. 'I was here yesterday. You saw me.'

'Well, then, it must have been the ghost,' said Melisande triumphantly. 'Bessie said they've heard all sorts of mysterious noises coming from upstairs lately. Cook said it was probably bats but Bessie thinks it's far too loud for that, and she's certain the place is haunted. All the maids are terrified—I dare say I should be myself if I had to sleep on the third floor.'

She then returned to her French composition and Barbara and Violet glanced at each other.

'We simply have to get up to the attics,' said Barbara in a low voice.

'But what about Miss Finch?' said Violet. 'Her room is at the bottom of the stairs. She'll see us if we try again.'

'She might not be there,' said Barbara. 'I'll just slip along and have a look.'

She returned a minute or two later, shaking her head.

'It's no good,' she said. 'She's in there with the door wide open, marking books. I shouldn't be surprised if she suspects we're up to something.'

To their annoyance, Miss Finch remained firmly in place for the rest of the evening, and when the bell rang for bed-time Barbara and Violet had no choice but to go up with the rest of the girls.

'Don't undress,' said Barbara. 'We'll have to do it tonight.'

'Can't it wait until tomorrow?' said Violet, whose initial enthusiasm for rebellion was rapidly wearing off.

'But what if she's hurt?' said Barbara. 'I'm sure she'd have come out by now if she could have. Listen, it won't take long at all, I'm sure of it. We'll just go up and have a quick look around, and if she's there we'll bring her down here or fetch help if we need to. It'll be as easy as anything.'

'But it'll be dark. Wouldn't it make more sense to tell one of the teachers about it instead?' said Violet.

'We've already tried. You've seen for yourself what Miss Finch thinks of our ideas. Why should any of the others listen to us when she won't? No,' said Barbara firmly, 'this is the only way.'

There was no deterring Barbara when she had a plan in her head, and so Violet reluctantly agreed. Barbara promised to wake her up at two o'clock or thereabouts, and shortly afterwards the lights went out in the Fourth Form dormitory, with two of the girls still fully dressed under the bedclothes, and one of them, at least, looking forward to a night-time adventure.

Chapter Twenty-Three

ALAS! For as the poet says, even the best laid plans may go awry. Barbara had gone to sleep, telling herself firmly several times to wake up at two o'clock, but when she did finally awaken and look at her watch, she found to her dismay that it was after five. If they were going to search the attics they would have to hurry before the servants got up and spotted them. She slipped out of bed as quietly as possible and shook Violet awake, and they both tiptoed out of the dorm. Within a very few minutes they were creeping along the third floor passage, listening carefully for the sound of anyone stirring, but all they could hear was snoring coming from one of the rooms. Barbara flashed her torch towards the end of the corridor and pointed. In a little recess to the right was a low, narrow door.

'There,' she whispered. 'It creaks, so be careful.'

She led the way to the door, turned the handle and pushed it open very slowly, but even so it emitted a low groan. They froze and listened, but no-one came. Behind the door the darkness was complete, and Violet clutched nervously at Barbara's arm.

'Don't leave me,' she said.

'Didn't you bring a torch?' said Barbara.

'I haven't got one,' said Violet.

Barbara rolled her eyes in the gloom but merely said, 'There are stairs here. I'll go first. Tread carefully.'

The stairs were steep and narrow and creaked a little, and they ascended as quietly as they could. At the top it was slightly less dark and the air was cooler and fresher, and as Barbara waved the torch around Violet saw that they had emerged into a large space under the roof of the building. As might have been expected, the place was full of stuff: broken chairs, old desks, piles of boxes and other assorted oddments that had been brought up here to be left and forgotten about.

'Don't walk too heavily,' said Barbara. 'Remember the servants are sleeping below.'

'There doesn't seem to be anything up here,' said Violet.

'No,' agreed Barbara, 'but I'll just take a quick look around in case she's asleep, or something.'

She took a few steps and swept the darkest corners of the room with her torch, but saw nothing.

'Shall we go down now?' said Violet, who was frightened but did not like to admit it.

'There's another room over there,' said Barbara. 'That's the way out onto the roof.'

Violet looked towards where she had pointed and saw another door in a far wall, and realized that this was not the only attic room. Barbara was already heading towards the door, and Violet followed hurriedly, stumbling over a broken stool as she did so.

'Shh!' hissed Barbara.

'Sorry,' whispered Violet, but Barbara was flapping at her to be quiet. They stopped and listened. Was it their imagination, or had there been an answering thump when Violet had made the noise? At that moment, Violet would quite happily have made a run for it back down the stairs, but Barbara was pressing on and so she had no choice but to follow or be left in the dark. They went through the door together and found themselves in a smaller room. This one was empty.

'That's the way out to the roof,' said Barbara, waving her torch at a small flight of steps with a door at the top. 'It's locked now so we can't get out.' She glanced about. 'There's nothing in here. The last room is through there. Oh!'

'What is it?' said Violet nervously.

'Look,' said Barbara. She crept across and shone her torch on a door of only five feet in height which was set into the very darkest corner of the opposite wall. Violet followed and gazed at the thing Barbara was indicating. It was the door handle, which had evidently come loose and fallen off. The two girls stared at each other and Barbara placed a finger over her lips. They listened, and as they did so they heard an unmistakable scraping sound coming from the other side, which made them both jump and clutch each other.

'Somebody's in there!' whispered Violet, terrified.

Even Barbara was quailing slightly by now. She hesitated, then took a deep breath, set her jaw and knocked gently. The scraping noise stopped immediately, to be replaced by utter silence.

'No answer,' she said.

Violet pulled herself together with an effort.

'You've probably terrified the life out of whoever it is,' she said. She tapped on the door and hissed, 'Florrie! Are you in there?'

There was a squeak of surprise and the sound of someone scrambling to their feet.

'Who's that?' came Florrie's quavering voice. 'Barbara, is that you?'

'Yes,' said Barbara in relief. 'How on earth did you get in there? We've been looking everywhere for you!'

'I can't get out,' said Florrie. 'The handle fell off the door and I've been stuck here for simply ages. I knocked and yelled but nobody came. Please get me out.'

'I'm trying,' said Barbara, who had picked up the door handle and was attempting vainly to put it back on. 'It's no use. Something's broken off here and it won't fit on. Can't you open it from your side?'

'Do you suppose I'd still be here if I could?' said Florrie, sounding exasperated. 'The whole thing fell apart when I shut the door and trapped me inside.'

'Just a second, then,' said Barbara.

'How are we going to get it open?' said Violet. 'That bit there is completely snapped.'

'We might break the door down,' suggested Barbara.

'I've already tried that,' said Florrie from the other side. 'It's no use. It's completely solid.'

'Then we'll need some tools to get this lock off,' said Violet. 'Where can we get them?'

Barbara thought for a second, then an idea came to her.

'William!' she said. 'Let's go and fetch William.'

'Your aunt's chauffeur?' said Violet. 'The American?'

'She's not my aunt, she's my godmother,' said Barbara. 'Listen, Flo,' she said through the door. 'We're going to get William to fix the door for us. We'll be back as soon as we can.'

'Can he be trusted?' said Florrie, and her voice sounded suddenly frightened.

'Of course he can,' said Barbara. 'Now, don't worry—we'll be back in a trice, I promise.'

In no time at all Barbara and Violet were hurrying across the lawn to the coach-house.

'We can't just barge in there,' said Barbara when they arrived. She scooped up a handful of gravel and threw it at the top window. Most of it missed, but some hit its target, and within a minute or two William appeared at the window, yawning and rubbing his eyes. Barbara beckoned vigorously and he nodded and turned away. Two minutes later he emerged from the building in his shirt-sleeves.

'What's all this?' he said. 'Oughtn't you two to be in bed?'

'We've found her, but the handle fell off and she's been there for days so you'll need to bring a screwdriver or something,' said Barbara breathlessly.

William raised his eyebrows and looked to Violet for a translation.

'Florrie is stuck in the attic,' she said. 'Could you help us get her out, please?'

'What were you doing in the attic at this time of night?' said William. 'I can't join in your tricks, Miss Barbara, you know that. I'll get into all kinds of trouble if I get caught.'

'It's not a trick, I promise,' said Barbara. 'Florrie's been missing for days and nobody seems to care because of Irina, so we went to look for her ourselves and now we've found her and she's locked in and needs our help. *Do* please come. If we go and get Miss Finch she'll just give us a terrible scolding for going up there, and then even if she does listen to us all she'll do is fetch you or someone else anyway, and by that time another few hours will have gone by and perhaps Flo will have starved to death by then. Besides, we promised her we'd be back in a minute.'

William looked at the two girls' worried faces and relented.

'All right, then,' he said. 'I'll come. But you'd better not be kidding me.'

The girls assured him of their sincerity, and he disappeared inside and returned, wearing his jacket this time, and carrying a small roll of tools and a torch, which he shoved in his pocket.

'The attics are up here, through the servants' quarters,' said Barbara, when they reached the stairs to the third floor. 'Be careful not to wake the kitchen-maids up.'

'I'm going to be in big trouble if they catch me up here,' muttered William, glancing about nervously.

'Well, then, keep quiet and they won't,' said Barbara.

They reached the door at the end of the third floor passage without incident, and climbed the attic stairs.

'Are you still there, Florrie?' said Barbara, knocking on the door of the end room.

'Where else would I be?' came an impatient voice.

'We've brought William. He's going to get the door open. You'd better stand back in case he has to kick it down.'

'No need for that,' said William, examining the lock by the light of his torch. 'I reckon a couple of minutes ought to do the job.'

He set to work, and within a very short time something clanged to the floor and the door swung open. They peered into the room and saw a white-faced and very grubby Florrie shielding her eyes against the light of their torches. She was holding something in her hand. It was a small but lethal-looking knife.

'Stay back!' she said.

Chapter Twenty-Four

ANGELA MARCHMONT HAD TAKEN the news of Edwards' murder in a very different light from Miss Bell, for it seemed to her that it had only complicated matters further. For the whole of Monday evening she reflected carefully on the events of the past few days, for she still had the strangest feeling that in all the confusion of Irina's return she had missed an important fact. But what was it? She was certain that if only she could see things from the right angle then all would become clear, but ten o'clock came and she was still none the wiser, so in the end she decided to go to bed. Perhaps the answer would come to her in the night.

On Tuesday morning she awoke before the dressing-bell, with the mystery still running through her mind and seemingly no closer to a solution. There was no possibility of getting back to sleep, so she got up and went downstairs. There were few people about at that hour, and she wandered out into the Quad and sat on a stone bench, intending to take advantage of the temporary peace and quiet before breakfast to try and put her thoughts in order.

The early morning air was cold, but she did not notice it as she gazed about her in the grey light and listened to the soothing sound of the trickling water from the fountain. Someone had left an exercise-book out on another bench across the Quad. It was the same bench favoured by Barbara and her friends, and Angela idly thought back to her first encounter with the girls. They seemed a kind and friendly set, which presumably explained why they had invited Irina to join them, for otherwise they appeared to have little in common with the Princess, whose reserved manner and apparent maturity in some respects sat oddly in this school of happy, jolly, innocent children.

Angela set herself to think about what had happened on Saturday. It had begun, of course, with their trip to Percham and their meeting with Irina and Mr. Everich, of whom Angela still harboured some suspicion, for she had been unable to think of any reason why he should have lied about the time of his journey from Vorgorod. Very well, then, assuming Everich was one of the criminals, what could explain his behaviour? Why had he bothered with the whole rigmarole of sending Irina a note and instructing her to come out to meet him in the middle of the night, when he might easily have spirited her away on Saturday afternoon? It made no sense at all. And once he had her in his clutches, why had he then returned to the school and insisted on questioning all her friends, when he ought to have disappeared himself? Again, it was inexplicable. After turning the question over in her mind for several minutes, Angela was forced to admit that perhaps her suspicions of Everich were unjustified, for leaving aside his initial lie, there was nothing to suggest that he was anything other than what he purported to be—an Intelligence man sent to protect the Princess from her enemies. In fact, he had behaved exactly as one would have expected after the girl went missing, exhibiting any amount of dismay and nervousness and attempting to find out what had happened to her.

With some reluctance, therefore, Angela abandoned her theory that Everich was the criminal. But if not he, then who? There was no doubt of Edwards the gardener's involvement, but he had not acted alone, for he had certainly not slit his own throat, and Irina was quite sure that she had heard the voice of another man in the house in which she had been held prisoner. Angela frowned. That was another thing: the mystery of the abduction itself. According to Henry Jameson, Princess Irina was in danger of being assassinated—and Henry Jameson was not in the habit of exaggerating for effect. If Henry said there was a threat, then he truly believed it himself. Why, then, had the kidnappers let Irina go once they had her? Surely the whole point of the abduction was to kill the girl and start a war in Morania. And yet they had left the door unlocked and allowed her to escape.

Yes, Irina's story had been a strange one, right enough. Angela tried to remember exactly what the Princess had said. There were one or two points in particular that had struck Angela at the time. One she might have been mistaken on, but another seemed most odd. Perhaps there was a perfectly good explanation for it all, but still, the whole story did not sit well with her.

A seagull swooped down and landed on the back of another bench, driven in by the cold wind. It was a magnificent bird, and it eyed Angela with disdain. Angela regarded it thoughtfully as another point came into her mind. Just then, the dressing-bell rang to signal the start of another school day and Angela made an effort to rouse herself from her reverie. Soon the girls would come down to breakfast, and then lessons would begin just as they did every other day. Irina had returned safely, and all was now well—except, of course, for the small fact that there was another missing girl—one who had been almost over-looked in all the excitement over the Princess. Angela frowned again. Florrie had not yet been found, as far as she knew. Where had she gone? And did her disappear-ance have anything to do with Irina's?

Angela suddenly realized that she was feeling cold, so she stood up, leaving her bench to the girls, and left the Quad through the arch. The first thing she saw was William's young friends, the twins, laughing as they ran hand in hand across the lawn. She stopped dead and stared at them.

'Oh, goodness me,' she said, astounded, for the most extraordinary idea had just come into her head. 'That can't be right, can it? No, of course it can't. Someone would have mentioned it by now, surely.'

But the idea had lodged itself firmly into her brain and would not go away, and so she forced herself to think through the thing slowly from the beginning. Yes—it would fit, of course it would! Some parts of the story were not clear to her, but the thing as a whole made perfect sense if looked at from this new angle. Of course, it meant that more than one person had been telling lies all along, but that was quite understandable in the circumstances. Could it really be true? The thing was quite extraordinary if it was, but certainly not so extraordinary as to be impossible. Poor Irina! It looked as though she had been betrayed by the very thing that was meant to protect her. How fright-ened she must have been! And still she was not safe.

Angela turned and ran back into the building. She must find Mr. Hesketh or Miss Bell immediately and ask them whether they knew anything, although she was almost certain they did not, for surely it would have come out by now. She went to Mr. Hesketh's room and then to the staff common-room, but the Latin master was nowhere to be found and nobody could tell her where he was. Then she went to Miss Bell's study. The headmistress was there, and greeted Mrs. Marchmont with a smile.

'Ah, Mrs. Marchmont,' she said. 'I suppose you will be leaving us—'

'Miss Bell, what exactly do you know about Princess Irina?' said Angela abruptly, without waiting for her to finish.

'I beg your pardon?' said Miss Bell in some surprise.

Angela was about to go on when they were interrupted by Miss Bell's secretary, who apologized profusely but said that His Excellency had arrived and wished to see the headmistress immediately. She was followed into the room by a young man of straight and stately bearing, who bowed his head to the two ladies and correctly identified the one in charge.

'I am Count Paul of Vorgorod,' he said to the head-mistress. 'And you are Miss Bell, yes?'

'Oh, Your Excellency,' said Miss Bell. 'I am so glad you have arrived. You will, of course, have heard the good news that Her Highness has been found safe and well.'

'I have indeed, just now,' said Count Paul. 'And I need not say that it is a profound relief to me to hear it. She was found last night, yes? I trust His Highness the Grand Duke has been informed?'

'Naturally,' said Miss Bell. 'We sent a telegram at once.'

'Good,' said Count Paul. 'Then the worry will be the less for him. He is still very sick, of course, and the recent concern over his daughter cannot have done him any good. I should like to speak to Her Highness as soon as possible, in private. She will no doubt be very anxious to hear news of her father.'

'But of course,' said Miss Bell. 'She will be at breakfast now. Mr. Everich and Mr. Hesketh have been charged with keeping an eye on her at all times.'

'Ah, yes, Everich,' said Count Paul, in a manner which suggested that Mr. Everich was about to have a stiff time of it.

'If you will come this way,' said the headmistress.

The two of them swept out of the room before Angela could say a word, leaving her in a state of some perplexity. There was evidently no use in trying to speak to Miss Bell at present. Perhaps Mr. Hesketh would be more amenable to hearing what she had to say, if she could find him. Angela left the study, intending to follow the headmistress and her illustrious guest to the dining-room, but was immediately waylaid by Barbara, who had come to look for her.

'Quick!' hissed Barbara. 'We've found Florrie, but she won't come out!'

'What?' said Angela in astonishment.

'Come on!' said Barbara, tugging at Angela's arm. 'Before someone sees us.'

Angela needed no further prompting.

'Where is she?' she said, as they hurried along the passage.

'We've put her in your room for now,' said Barbara. 'She's been trapped in the attic since Saturday night and we had to get William to get her out. But she didn't want to come out at first and waved a knife at us, so we had to spend ages persuading her. She won't say anything and won't come out of your room. She just keeps insisting she wants to speak to Mr. Hesketh. But he can't leave Irina, can he? So she'll just have to make do with you instead.'

'Why was she in the attic?'

'I don't know, she won't say. She's being awfully odd,' said Barbara.

They arrived at Angela's room and Barbara knocked at the door three times then twice. Violet answered it.

'Where's Mr. Hesketh?' she said.

'He's with Irina,' said Barbara. 'I could only find Angela.'

They entered and Angela saw Florrie sitting on the edge of the bed, looking pale and wary. She did not seem especially pleased to see the new arrival.

'Mr. Hesketh can't leave Irina,' said Barbara, 'so I brought you Angela. She's working for Intelligence too.'

'Is she?' said Florrie in some surprise.

'Yes, so you can speak to her instead,' said Barbara.

Florrie shook her head.

'I need to speak to Mr. Hesketh,' she said stubbornly. 'He's the only one I can trust.'

'You're being awfully strange,' said Barbara. 'Why won't you say anything?'

'I think I know,' said Angela.

Florrie looked up suddenly.

'What do you know?' she said.

'Why, that you're not who you say you are,' said Angela. 'I am right, aren't I, Your Highness?'

Chapter Twenty-Five

'*WHAT?*' said Barbara and Violet together.

Angela had held her breath for a second after hazarding her wild supposition, but one look at Florrie told her she had hit the mark.

'Don't you think it's about time you told your friends?' she said.

'What are you talking about?' said Barbara.

'You're not a princess too, are you?' said Violet to Florrie.

'No,' said Angela. 'There's just the one princess as far as I know, and this is she.'

'You've got it all wrong, Angela,' said Barbara. 'This is Florrie Evans.'

But Florrie was looking at Angela.

'How did you know?' she said.

'What? You don't mean to say she's right, do you?' said Barbara. 'You can't be a princess. Why, look at you—you're filthy!'

Florrie drew herself up.

'I *am* a princess,' she said proudly. 'My name is Irina Florentyna Aleksandra Elena Ivanoveti of Morania.'

The girls stared.

'But—' said Barbara.

'But—' said Violet.

Despite herself, Florrie looked rather pleased with the effect she had created.

'But you're just a *girl*,' said Barbara at last. 'You drew a picture of Miss Devlin with a moustache in the back of my Geography book. You came up on the roof and threw eggs at Mr. Penkridge and I took the blame. Princesses don't *do* that sort of thing.'

'I know,' said Florrie, a little sadly. 'We don't, as a rule. It was awfully sporting of you to say you threw the eggs. I shan't forget it, I promise.' She looked up at Mrs. Marchmont. 'Has there been any news of my father?' she said. 'I've been worried sick about him. Is he—is he still alive?'

'He is,' said Angela. 'As a matter of fact, I believe he is much better.'

Florrie clasped her hands together and looked as though she hardly dared believe it.

'Are you quite sure?' she said. 'Mr. Hesketh said things looked very bad for him.'

'I gather the situation is not as desperate as it first appeared,' replied Angela. 'He is very unwell at present, of course, but he is receiving the best of care and I understand he is expected to recover.'

Florrie burst into tears.

'Oh! I'm so glad,' was all she said, and had Angela had any lingering doubts about Florrie's real identity, they were now dispelled. The girl they had thought was Irina had shown not the slightest interest in the Grand Duke's fate when she returned, but Florrie's first concern was her father.

'But if you're the Princess, then who is the other Irina?' said Violet, while Florrie blew her nose on a dirty handkerchief and pulled herself together with an effort. 'And why does everybody think she's you?'

'She was sent with me to protect me,' said Florrie. 'My father had the idea when he found out that someone was plotting against us. I was coming to school anyway, and British Intelligence knew about it, and about the threat, but Father wouldn't let me go without additional protection, and so he sent her to pretend to be me, as a kind of decoy. Nobody knows who I am in Morania, you see, and if it happened to come out that I'd gone to school in England and anyone wanted to find me, then they'd think Natalia was me.'

'Natalia? Is that her name?' said Barbara. 'But who is she?'

'Natalia Everich,' said Florrie. 'She is Raul Everich's wife.'

'Ah!' said Angela, as the other two exclaimed in surprise. That explained why the fake Irina had seemed so much older than her years: she was not a schoolgirl at all, but a grown woman. 'But Florrie, who knew about all this? Miss Bell and Mr. Hesketh were not informed, I take it.'

'No,' said Florrie. 'My father thought it better to tell as few people as possible, so only he and I, and my cousin Paul and the Everichs knew about it. If anyone else had known they'd have felt bound to keep a close eye on me, and then it would have been obvious who I was. And I wanted to be treated like a normal girl too, so I was happy enough to agree to it. The two of us started at Wakeley Court at the same time, but Natalia arrived by motor-car with an official escort from the British Government, while I came up on the train from London with a woman from the Moranian Embassy who didn't know who I was—only that

I was the daughter of someone high up in the Civil Service and was to be looked after.'

'I say, it was rather brave of Irina to impersonate you,' said Barbara. 'Especially since it ended up in her being kidnapped. It's just her good luck that they let her go when they might easily have killed her. She must have convinced them somehow that she wasn't you.'

'What do you mean?' said Florrie, staring. 'She wasn't kidnapped, was she?'

'Yes,' said Barbara, 'and that's probably why nobody found you sooner—everyone was far too concerned with finding her because they thought *she* was the real Princess Irina. Nobody even noticed you were missing until yesterday. It's a good thing Violet and I decided to start a search for you, or you might never have been found.'

'But I don't understand. Who took Natalia?' said Florrie.

'Edwards the gardener. Oh! Isn't that funny?' said Barbara, suddenly remembering. 'I *said* he was a foreign spy, didn't I? And you told me off for scaring Irina.'

Florrie said nothing, but there was a puzzled frown on her face.

'So why *were* you in the attic?' said Violet. 'Did the kidnappers lock you in?'

'Of course not,' said Florrie. 'I ran in there and the handle fell off, just as you saw.'

'Is that when you were running away from them?' said Barbara. 'Did you and Irina go out together?'

'Yes,' said Florrie. 'We arranged to meet outside at half-past two and go to the summer-house together, but in the struggle we got separated and I ran back into the building. I only meant to hide for a little while, but then I got stuck and couldn't get out. So Natalia went missing, did she?'

'Yes, but she's back now. I don't know exactly what happened—Angela can probably tell you that.'

Florrie turned her eyes questioningly towards Angela, who said:

'She told rather an odd story about being taken to a house in Percham and held prisoner. She says she escaped yesterday evening when her captors left the door unlocked.'

Florrie snorted.

'Rot!' she said. 'I don't believe a word of it. She probably said it just to get herself out of trouble.'

'That's hardly kind, when she put herself in danger for your sake,' said Barbara, who was very fair-minded.

'Put herself in danger for my sake?' said Florrie. 'Don't be an ass, Barbara. Haven't you been listening?'

'Of course I have,' said Barbara. 'But I haven't understood much yet. Do you mean Irina was lying about where she was?'

'Yes, you idiot,' said Florrie. 'She's been lying all along. She came here to betray me, and she very nearly managed it.'

Chapter Twenty-Six

ANGELA LEFT Florrie in the care of Barbara and Violet, with strict instructions to allow no-one to enter the room, while she hurried downstairs to fetch Mr. Hesketh. They had all been kept in the dark for far too long now, and it was vital that he be informed immediately of the real situation. The girl they had believed to be Irina was not the Princess at all, but the wife of Morania's Head of Intelligence, who had lured Florrie into a trap, presumably with the intention of killing her. Only Florrie's natural wariness and quick thinking had allowed her to escape. Had she not then become trapped in the attic, the Everichs might now be safely under arrest.

Florrie's story was simple enough. After the attempt on the Grand Duke's life, she had been all for going straight to Mr. Hesketh and confessing her real identity to him, for she wanted to get back to Morania as quickly as possible to be at her father's bedside. But Natalia Everich had persuaded her not to do it, saying that there was danger all around, and that it was more important than ever for the secret to be kept. Raul would be here tomorrow, she said, and he would take them home, but in the meantime the assassins were still at large, and so it was vital that the Princess remain in hiding for the present. Florrie was unhappy at this, but obeyed, since, after all, Natalia *was* there to protect her, and presumably knew what she was doing.

On Saturday Everich arrived, but Florrie was unable to speak to him for more than a minute or two. He told her to be patient, and that she should hear from him before the day was out. He then went off to Percham with Natalia—presumably, as it turned out, for the purposes of putting the finishing touches to the plot against the Princess. Late that afternoon Natalia returned from Percham with a note from Everich. The note said that they were all to return to Morania that night, and that Florrie must come out to the summer-house with Natalia to meet Everich there. She was not to bring anything since she was going to be smuggled out of the country and there would be no room for luggage. This all seemed rather odd to Florrie, who still did not understand why they should not tell Mr. Hesketh and employ the assistance of British Intelligence, and so perhaps she was more suspicious than she might otherwise have been. She decided to take her own precautions, and before she crept out of the dorm concealed in her sleeve a knife which had been a parting present from her father.

She met Natalia as instructed, and they went to the appointed meeting-place together. Florrie's feeling that something was wrong intensified as they walked, for Natalia was nervous and on edge, and gave only short answers to Florrie's questions. When they arrived at the summer-house Natalia stood back to allow Florrie to enter first, whereupon Florrie smelled a rat and suggested they wait outside. Natalia urged her on, saying that they had better hurry, or Miss Bell would wake up and notice she was missing and then the plan would be ruined. She was so insistent that Florrie went in, and was immediately set upon by two men, one of whom tried to clap a handkerchief drenched in something sweet-smelling over her nose. Unfortunately for him, Florrie had been half-expecting something of the sort and had her knife at the ready, which she stuck as hard as she could into his hand. He yelled and loosened his hold, while the other man retreated for an instant at the sight of the knife, giving her the opportunity to escape. She shot out of the summer-house and back towards the school building, intending to raise the alarm, with one of the men in pursuit. She glanced behind her, saw the moonlight glinting off his fair hair, and knew for certain then that it was Everich and that she had been betrayed.

She had thought she would be safe when she reached the school building, but to her horror he followed her inside, into a wing well away from all the teachers. She crouched behind a cupboard in one of the corridors, listening to her pursuer open first one classroom door then another in search of her, and wondered where she might go, but in her fear the only place she could think of was the attic. Everich was getting closer, and so she waited for him to open another door and under cover of the sound made a dive for the stairs across the way. She reached the attic, congratulating herself on having shaken him off, and intending to come out in daylight when there were plenty of people about, but to her dismay, when she shut the little door behind her the handle came off in her hand, and she found herself trapped. And there she had stayed until Barbara and Violet had come to find her, oblivious to all the uproar over the disappearance of the fake princess. Now she was safe—or would be once the Everichs had been unmasked as the traitors they were and put under arrest.

Angela ran to the classroom where she knew Mr. Hesketh would shortly be taking the Fifth for Latin, and found him just about to begin. Natalia Everich was sitting at the front of the class, her expression inscrutable. She looked up as Angela entered.

'I beg your pardon, Mr. Hesketh,' said Angela, 'but I have an urgent message for you.'

Hesketh gave a glance at Natalia, and came out, shutting the door behind him.

'What is it?' he said.

Angela explained the situation in a few words, and he clutched the door handle and went pale.

'If I didn't know better, Mrs. Marchmont, I should say you were joking,' he said, aghast.

'It's no joke, I'm afraid,' said Angela.

Hesketh's mouth opened and closed once or twice, but no words came out. Finally he found his voice and swore inventively, much to the astonishment of a passing First Form girl, who squeaked and ran away. He apologized immediately.

'That's quite all right,' said Angela, secretly entertained at the sight of the even-tempered Mr. Hesketh losing his head. 'It was a surprise to me too. But there's no doubt of it: we have been protecting the wrong girl all along.'

Mr. Hesketh waved his hands.

'Those Moranians!' he exclaimed. 'Why must they make things so unnecessarily complicated, with all this cloak and dagger stuff? If we'd known from the beginning then we might have done something about it, but instead they've made fools of us all *and* put their Princess in danger.'

'Well, it would have been a good plan had the Everichs been trustworthy,' said Angela fairly. 'It was just Florrie's bad luck that her father happened to choose the wrong people to look after her.'

'So it's Mrs. Everich, is it? That little—' said Hesketh. He broke off without completing the epithet. 'Why, she's had us all out scouring the whole of Norfolk for her, and arresting perfectly innocent men for no good reason.'

'Shh! We mustn't let her know we suspect her,' said Angela. 'The police will have to deal with her and her husband, but in the meantime you'd better come and see Florrie. It's lucky for us that Count Paul has arrived. We might have had some difficulty in convincing people that she is the real Princess, but he must surely know of the deception.'

'Yes,' said Hesketh. 'I wonder why he has said nothing.'

Just then they saw the Count himself, accompanied by Miss Bell, approaching them. The Count looked very serious, and to judge by the headmistress's face it appeared as though she had just heard some terrible news.

'Oh, Mr. Hesketh!' she exclaimed. 'His Excellency has just told me the most extraordinary story. It appears we have all been labouring under a terrible misapprehension.'

'Yes,' said Hesketh. 'Mrs. Marchmont has just told me about it. I know Irina is not the real Princess.'

The two newcomers both regarded Angela in surprise.

'But how did you know, Mrs. Marchmont?' said Miss Bell.

'Mainly because Irina's English is not good enough for someone who was supposed to have spent all her childhood years in England,' said Angela. 'There were one or two other things, but when Irina came back and Florrie didn't, it occurred to me that perhaps we had been looking for the wrong person.'

'Yes,' said Count Paul. 'I deeply regret having deceived everyone, but His Highness the Grand Duke and I thought it was the best way to keep his daughter safe. Evidently we were wrong, for she has disappeared all the same. I have spoken to Natalia Everich this morning and she can tell me nothing of where Her Highness has gone. It is a complete mystery, and I am beside myself with fear for her fate.'

'There's no need for that, Your Excellency,' said Angela. 'She's upstairs in my room, quite safe, if a little grubby and probably very hungry.'

'What?' exclaimed Count Paul. 'You are joking, surely.'

Angela swiftly assured him that she was quite serious and explained where Florrie had been, and a smile of great relief spread across his face, which was quickly followed by a frown.

'Then—but—does she know who attacked her?' he said.

'It was Everich,' replied Mr. Hesketh. 'It appears that he and his wife have been playing a part all along.'

'Everich?' said Count Paul in wonder. 'But he is our most trusted man.'

'Not any more,' said Hesketh dryly.

The Count opened his mouth then closed it again.

'Please, I should like to see Her Highness at once,' he said. 'Her *real* Highness, that is.'

'Certainly,' said Angela. 'I left her in my room with Barbara and Violet, who rescued her from the attic. I think Barbara was going to fetch her some food from the kitchen.'

Abandoning the Fifth Form to their own devices, the four of them hurried up to Mrs. Marchmont's room. As soon as they arrived at the top of the stairs, however, they knew that something had gone very wrong, for the first thing they saw was Violet Smedley running towards them along the passage, white-faced and terrified.

'Everich's got Florrie!' she exclaimed when she saw them. 'He's got a gun. Quick, you must catch him!'

Chapter Twenty-Seven

BARBARA ARRIVED JUST at that moment, carrying some rolls and butter.

'What's going on?' she said in astonishment, looking from one horrified face to another.

Violet sank to the ground and wrung her hands.

'It's all my fault!' she cried. 'He knocked—three then two, just as we arranged, and I thought it was you, so I opened the door. Florrie had put her knife down and she didn't have a chance to grab it before he got hold of her and dragged her off. Didn't you see them when you were coming up?'

'No,' managed Hesketh, who looked as though he were on the point of combustion.

'Then they must have gone down the other staircase,' said Miss Bell.

Hesketh said no more but ran off, followed by Miss Bell and Count Paul.

'But how did he know how to knock?' said Angela.

Barbara looked crestfallen.

'He must have been up here and overheard me when I

went to get some food,' she said. 'As I came out of the room I said something like, "Don't forget, three knocks then two." I expect I was speaking rather loudly.'

'Dear me,' said Angela. 'Did he say anything?' she said to Violet.

'Yes, but it was in Moranian and I couldn't understand it. He pointed a gun at me and grabbed Florrie and took her away almost before I knew what was happening. Where do you suppose he's going to take her?'

'I don't know,' said Angela grimly. She did not say that she feared for Florrie's life, but there was no need, for the girls understood it well enough.

The three of them stared at one another for a second, then of one accord turned and ran down the stairs.

'Stay here,' Angela told the girls as they arrived in the main corridor. 'Or better still, go to your lesson. There's nothing you can do to help and it's best you don't get in the way.'

She did not suppose there was much she could do either, but she intended to try all the same. She left the building and ran as fast as she could down to the coach-house in search of William. She found him peering into the inner workings of the school charabanc in company with an old fellow who was evidently as deaf as a post, for they were conversing in loud bellows and gestures.

'Quick!' she cried. 'Everich has run off with Florrie Evans, and I'm awfully afraid he's going to kill her.'

William was instantly at attention.

'Where did they go?' he said.

'I don't know yet,' said Angela. 'Mr. Hesketh followed them. I don't know if Everich expects to get far, but he has a gun and he's obviously very dangerous, so we'll have to be careful. I doubt there's much I can do, but I'm supposed to be here to help so I'd better try and do *something*, at least.'

'Well, what are we waiting for?' said William. 'Let's go and find them.'

He left the old coachman without so much as a good-bye, and the two of them hurried across the lawn and back towards the school building. They were not more than halfway there when they spotted some sort of disturbance taking place ahead of them and stopped short.

'There they are,' said Angela.

From where they stood they could see a man with light-coloured hair, leading—or possibly dragging—a girl along the path towards a smart motor-car, which was stationed a little way down the drive.

'He's going to take her away in the car,' said Angela.

'How's he going to drive it, if she doesn't want to be driven?' said William. 'Not much use in having a gun when you're trying to keep your eyes on the road.'

They watched as the two reached the motor-car and Everich opened the door and bundled Florrie in. Sure enough, he had barely climbed in himself when the door on the other side burst open and Florrie tumbled out and onto the ground. Everich leapt out after her and hauled her up roughly by the collar. He shook her hard and appeared to clip her on the side of the head with some-thing, and they heard her cry out.

'Hey!' said William indignantly. 'He hit her with the gun! That—' He broke off, as he remembered Angela's presence.

Everich had evidently reached the same conclusion about driving the girl away as William had, but he was not about to give up. Florrie was still struggling and he clipped her across the head again. This time she fell senseless to the ground, and Angela gave a little gasp. Everich picked

Florrie up and slung her over his shoulder as though she weighed nothing, and set off down the drive at a brisk pace.

'There's Mr. Hesketh!' said Angela.

It was indeed the Latin master, who had shed his gown and mortar-board and was running down the drive after the fugitive, holding what looked like a gun in his hand. Everich heard him coming and turned, and from where Angela and William stood they could see him gesticulating towards Florrie with his own pistol. Hesketh fell back warily, and Everich continued on his way. It was not possible for Hesketh to get a good shot at him, for the unconscious Florrie was draped over him, and any bullet fired would hit her before it hit Everich.

Angela put her hand in her pocket and was reassured by the presence there of her own gun.

'Quick!' she said to William. 'Let's go back this way. If we go through the woods we might be able to cut him off by the gates, or at least see where he goes.'

They retreated the way they had come, went past the coach-house—where the old coachman did not seem to have noticed that William was missing and was still bellowing away—and entered the path that led through the trees to the road. They followed it for a little distance, and then Angela said:

'Here, we can cut through the trees this way. We'd better be quiet now.'

'What are we going to do if we find them, ma'am?' said William.

'I don't know,' said Angela. 'I rather hope that Mr. Hesketh is following them down the drive. We might be able to distract Everich while Hesketh gets Florrie. Perhaps you ought to take my gun, just in case.'

'Keep it. You're a better shot than I am,' said William,

as they turned from the path and set forth through the trees.

Meanwhile, the Fifth were having a most exciting morning of it. After twiddling their thumbs for twenty minutes waiting for Mr. Hesketh to come and start the Latin lesson, they had been getting rather bored, and one or two of them had begun to gaze idly out of the window. As they did so, they saw a man with very light-coloured hair dragging a struggling girl along the path towards the drive. There were several exclamations of astonishment, and everyone looked up.

'Why, it's Florrie!' said someone.

'What on earth is she doing with that man?' said someone else.

Just then, another man hurried past.

'It's Mr. Hesketh!' cried Sarah. 'And he's carrying a gun!'

Everyone gasped, and as one the entire class rose and ran to the window. There was much scuffling and shoving as everybody tried to get the best view.

'What on earth is going on?' said the first girl.

Nobody knew, but it was quite certain that neither hell nor high water would drag them away from the window until they had received a satisfactory explanation, and so no-one noticed as Natalia Everich rose from her seat and slipped out of the classroom. In the entrance-hall she bumped into Miss Bell and Count Paul.

'Irina! What are you doing out of lessons? Go back to your classroom immediately,' said Miss Bell, who was in a state of some confusion and had momentarily forgotten who was who and what was happening.

Natalia ignored the headmistress and addressed Count Paul in rapid Moranian. He replied coldly and turned to go outside, but she ran to him and grasped his sleeve, and he had no choice but to listen. She threw her arms up and spoke to him in an imploring tone, and at last he nodded curtly and they hurried out of the building together, leaving Miss Bell in greater perplexity than ever.

Outside, Barbara and Violet had ignored Angela's instructions to go to their lesson, and were watching the scene in wide-eyed horror. Miss Finch spotted them and hurried out.

'What do you think you are doing?' she snapped. 'You are supposed to be in class. Get back inside at once! This will be another black mark for you.'

'Oh, bother the black mark,' retorted Violet. 'You can give me two if you like. Florrie's our friend, and we're staying here until we know she's safe.'

Miss Finch was so astounded at the normally well-behaved Violet's rudeness that she was left briefly speechless. Barbara cast an impressed glance at her friend.

'I'm terribly sorry, Miss Finch,' she said. 'Violet is very upset about Florrie. I'm sure she didn't mean to be rude.'

Violet opened her mouth to earn herself another black mark and probably also a week's worth of detentions, but Barbara elbowed her in the ribs and she shut it again. Luckily for both girls, Miss Bell arrived just then in a great state, and swept Miss Finch away, leaving them to watch as Everich disappeared out of sight, followed by Mr. Hesketh and shortly afterwards Count Paul and Natalia Everich. Violet reached for Barbara's hand and clutched it, and they stared at one another in dismay.

Down in the woods, Angela and William were creeping as quietly as they could through the trees towards the school drive.

'Where do you suppose he's going?' whispered William.

'I don't know,' said Angela, 'but he can't keep carrying her forever. Assuming he didn't kill her with that blow to the head, she's bound to wake up sooner or later, and then what will he do?'

'I thought the whole idea was to kill her,' said William.

'Yes, I thought so too,' said Angela. 'As a matter of fact, I don't know why he hasn't done it yet. Perhaps he has some other plan we know nothing about.'

'Shh!' said William suddenly, and they froze. 'Who's that?'

The trees were thinner here and the road was in view ahead of them, and in the silence they could hear a voice.

'It's Mr. Hesketh,' said Angela.

They crept on until they found a thick clump of trees behind which to hide and observe what was happening. They had emerged close to the school gates; tall, brick pillars surmounted by fierce stone dragons. Here, Everich had stopped, and had set down his burden to rest with her feet on the ground, while he kept an arm around her waist and made sure her body was placed between his and Hesketh's gun. Florrie appeared to be regaining consciousness, for they heard her utter a low moan. Angela was relieved—as was Mr. Hesketh, it appeared, for they heard him call:

'Look, she's alive. Let her go now and we can look after her. There's no sense in your continuing with this ridiculous scheme. The Grand Duke is expected to make a full recovery. What's the use in killing the Princess?'

'I will not speak to you,' replied Everich imperiously. 'I will speak only to His Excellency. I see him coming behind you. He knows what I have to say. Let me speak to him. I must have guarantees, for I fear I have been misled.'

Angela and William glanced at one another and crept a little closer to the road. From where she stood, Angela could now see Count Paul striding down the drive towards the little group, with Natalia Everich hurrying along behind him. The two of them came up to where Hesketh was standing and stopped. There followed an exchange in Moranian between the two men, in which Count Paul appeared to be pleading with his former Head of Intelligence. Everich replied in a flinty voice and was evidently immovable on something, for he shook his head several times. Count Paul took a step towards him, and immediately Everich gripped the half-conscious Florrie to him and pointed the pistol at her head. The Count retreated hurriedly, speaking in tones intended to mollify.

Then Natalia stepped forward and began to speak. She raised her hands to heaven and spoke beseechingly, and for a moment Everich seemed to soften, for he spoke to her gently and with a smile. She sighed and gazed at him fondly, then stepped forward. Everich let go of Florrie and then, still with a smile playing over his face, raised his gun and shot his wife, who fell to the ground.

To say that the onlookers were shocked would be an understatement, but Count Paul and Mr. Hesketh had not even time to cry out in horror before there was another loud report and Raul Everich, too, dropped where he stood.

'What on earth—' said Mr. Hesketh.

Angela and William stepped out from the clump of trees. Angela's revolver was still in her hand, and she put it back in her pocket as she bent over Florrie, who was sitting on the road, groggy but conscious.

'Is he dead?' she said over her shoulder to William.

'Yes, ma'am,' said William. 'Quite dead. That was a good shot.'

'What about Natalia?'

Mr. Hesketh had quickly recovered himself and was crouching next to Natalia Everich.

'She's still alive,' he said, after checking for a pulse. 'We had better call a doctor. I beg your pardon, Mrs. March-mont, but was that you—' He broke off.

'Yes, I shot him,' she said, only half-attending, for she was concerned about Florrie. 'How is your head?' she said kindly. 'Do you think you can walk back to the school? If not, perhaps your cousin can carry you.'

'No!' said Florrie suddenly. 'Don't let him near me!'

'What do you mean?' said Angela.

Count Paul had stepped forward and was hovering about in concern.

'I mean he's a traitor like the others!' said Florrie.

Shaking off Angela's attempts to help, she struggled to her feet and stood, her head proudly erect, every inch the princess, glaring at the Count.

'What did you mean by it, Paul?' she said to him. 'How could you betray my father and me in that way? Did you hope to take power, just like the others? I thought you better than they. Obviously I was wrong.'

Count Paul looked taken aback. He began to say some-thing in Moranian, but she cut him short.

'Speak English,' she commanded. 'I want everyone to hear what you have to say. You were behind this whole thing, weren't you? The attack on my father and the plot to kill me.'

'Why, Irina, my little cousin, how can you accuse me of such a thing?' said Count Paul. He attempted to laugh, but Angela saw that he was pale and there was perspiration on his brow. 'My loyalty to you both is true and cannot be doubted. The Grand Duke has been as a father to me, and I have loved you as a sister. I—'

'Then what did Everich mean just now when he said the plan had changed?' said Florrie. 'I'm not stupid—I can understand well enough. He told me he was supposed to kill me, but that you telegraphed on Sunday afternoon and told him not to do it after all, and he was worried he'd been cheated. Why did you change your mind?'

'I don't know what you mean,' said Count Paul nervously. 'Everich was the traitor, not I. Your father sent me to bring you back safely, and that is what I mean to do.'

'Let us see what Natalia has to say—if she wakes up, that is,' said Florrie coolly. 'I am sure she will be able to tell us more. Mr. Hesketh,' she said, turning to the Latin master, 'I should like you to have this man arrested. I suspect him of plotting against the throne of Morania.'

At that, Count Paul turned and began to run.

'Er—' said Mr. Hesketh, who was struggling with matters of diplomatic etiquette, having never before been instructed by a princess—let alone one who still owed him a Latin translation—to arrest a count. Fortunately, William had no such qualms.

'Oh, no you don't,' he said, and gave chase. The result was a foregone conclusion, for the Count got no more than about twenty yards before William brought him down to the ground and pinned his arms behind his back.

'You'd better have the gun,' said Angela, as the two of them returned, Count Paul struggling and with a streak of mud down his face. William took the revolver and the Count regarded it warily and subsided.

'I do apologize, Your Excellency,' said Hesketh. 'Perhaps this is a misunderstanding that can be easily cleared up. However, Her Highness—' He glanced at Florrie uncomfortably.

'There's no misunderstanding,' said Florrie. 'He tried to have me killed.' She stepped up to the Count, and before anybody could stop her, spat at him. He flinched, but said nothing.

'Go and lock him in my room for now,' said Hesketh. William nodded and marched Count Paul away.

'We had better get some help for Irina—Natalia, I mean,' said Angela. 'Perhaps you could carry her back to the school, Mr. Hesketh. Can you walk, do you think, Florrie?'

'Yes,' said Florrie. There was a catch in her voice, and Angela saw tears in her eyes.

'You poor thing. You've had rather a time of it, haven't you?' she said.

'He was like a brother to me,' said Florrie with a little sob. 'Why must they all betray us?'

Angela wanted to say something but could find no words to comfort the girl. But Florrie did not need her sympathy. She pulled herself together quickly.

'This will hit Father hard,' she said. 'I must be everything to him in future. I should like to go inside now.'

Hesketh lifted up Natalia Everich with some difficulty, and Florrie took Angela's arm, and they all returned slowly up the drive towards the school, leaving the body of the dead assassin to lie where it had fallen.

Chapter Twenty-Eight

'Goodness, how these Moranians do like to make things complicated,' said Mr. Hesketh, as he put down the telephone late that afternoon. 'I prefer a quiet life, myself—but then I don't have a country to rule, so I suppose it's easier for me.'

'Then Count Paul really is guilty, is he?' said Angela.

'It rather looks like it. As far as I understand it, his original intention was to have both father and daughter assassinated and then seize the throne, and so he laid the groundwork by spreading a rumour that the Krovodanians were planning such an attempt. That way, when he *did* take power he could blame the murders on Krovodar and have an excuse to invade the country. There's nothing like a successful war to detract attention from the legitimacy of one's own claim to power, and Count Paul knew that very well.'

'But the attempt on the Grand Duke failed,' said Angela.

'Yes—much to Count Paul's dismay, no doubt. Apparently the old man had no suspicion of who was really behind it, but when he found out that his daughter had gone missing—the real Irina, I mean, not the fake one—he promised Count Paul her hand in marriage if he brought her back. Since his first attempt to take power had failed, this seemed as good a way as any for the Count to get his hands on the throne, and he knew from Everich that Florrie had escaped and was in hiding somewhere, so he telegraphed to say that the plan had changed and that Florrie was not to be killed, and then came to England hot foot to find her and carry her back.

'Unfortunately for the Count, it appears that he had rather rashly promised Everich a position as chief minister in his new government, but with the Grand Duke still alive this was no longer possible. Everich was greatly disappointed when he found out, and wanted a guarantee that he would receive at least *some* sort of reward for his efforts, and that's why he ran off with the Princess. He intended to use her as an inducement to Count Paul to give him what he wanted.'

'That is, he threatened to kill her if he didn't get it,' said Angela. 'It's a good thing he was stopped. Anyone who can shoot his own wife in cold blood like that is evidently a very dangerous man. Why did he do it?'

'She saw the game was up and was trying to persuade him to hand over Florrie, I gather,' said Hesketh. 'I think at that point Everich saw her as merely an obstacle in his way and decided on the spur of the moment to be rid of her.'

Angela shuddered.

'I confess I found him rather frightening, myself,' she said. 'I take it he killed Edwards, too.'

'Yes,' said Hesketh. 'Edwards was another accomplice who had outlived his usefulness, and so had to be put out of the way.'

'Where *did* Irina—Natalia—go on Saturday night, by the way?' said Angela. 'Have the police found out yet?'

'Ah, yes,' said Hesketh. 'We made rather a blunder there. It appears that she and Edwards drove to Percham, where Everich was renting a little cottage by the harbour, and stayed there in the guise of Swiss tourists—it was easy enough for them to fool us that way, since we were searching for a fifteen-year-old schoolgirl, not a twenty-year-old woman. They even spoke to the police and tried to send them off on the wrong scent by saying they had heard a motor-boat out to sea. Presumably the idea was to make us think Irina had been taken abroad.'

'Yes, I did think Natalia's original story wasn't entirely convincing,' said Angela. 'Quite apart from anything else, she made a mistake by telling us she didn't know Edwards' name and then mentioning it shortly afterwards. That's partly what made me suspect her. But why did she come back?'

'She was never meant to disappear in the first place,' said Hesketh. 'It was only panic that made her run off to Percham with Edwards, after the attempt on Florrie went wrong. Of course, Everich had to play along and pretend he really believed the Princess was missing, while he decided how best to act in order to find the real Irina. He was still determined to get hold of Florrie, and I think he decided to bring Natalia out of hiding in the hope that she would be able to convince everyone she knew nothing of the plot and lure Florrie out, somehow. At any rate, she was no use to him stuck in a cottage miles away—especially once he had disposed of his other accomplice, Edwards, and so he cooked up a story for her and instructed her to return to the school.'

'It was a clever plan, though,' said Angela. 'Had it

worked, we'd never even have known the Princess was missing.'

'Yes,' agreed Hesketh. 'It was an ingenious idea, right enough, and it was only made possible in the first place because the Grand Duke tried to be cunning and sent his daughter here incognito. That extra touch made it easy for the plotters. I believe the plan was to lure Florrie outside and away from the school, kill her and dump her body some-where—probably in the sea. Then Everich would take the fake Irina back to Morania, still in the guise of the Princess, to claim the throne from her dead father. Once they were back home, of course, Irina would resume her identity as Natalia Everich. Eventually the news would filter back to Britain that Princess Irina had disappeared or died, and nobody would associate her disappearance with the missing schoolgirl Florrie Evans, whose parents would turn out to be untraceable. Since Count Paul would be ruler of Morania by then, the whole thing would be covered up and the Mora-nians wouldn't have to deal with any bothersome spluttering from our Foreign Office about assassinations on British soil.'

'How is Natalia, by the way?' said Angela.

'It's touch and go,' said Hesketh. 'Luckily the bullet missed her major organs, but it was still enough to do her rather a lot of damage. It will be some time before we can speak to her, if she does survive.'

'It all makes me very glad not to be a princess,' said Angela. 'Poor Florrie! It must have been a dreadful shock to her to find out that the people who were supposed to be protecting her were in fact plotting her death.'

'She's a princess, and a Moranian one at that,' said Hesketh. 'They're used to that sort of thing. We have had about twenty telegrams from the Grand Duke this after-noon, commanding us to lock her in the dorm until someone can be found to take her home. She sent him one back in reply. It was in Moranian but it was rather long and I imagine told him exactly what she thought of that idea.'

'She is certainly a remarkably self-possessed young woman,' said Angela. 'It's not every girl who would have the foresight to carry a knife around with her.'

'Yes—I think if anyone deserves credit for saving Florrie's life it's Florrie herself,' said Hesketh dryly. 'The rest of us made rather a bad fist of it.'

'Well, we did our best,' said Angela. 'And considering we were trying to protect the wrong person through no fault of our own, I don't think we did too badly.'

'True,' said Hesketh. 'By the way, Mrs. Marchmont, I take back what I said about a woman with a gun being the next best thing to a man. If I ever find myself in another tricky spot, I should be more than happy to have you—and your gun—by my side.'

'Why, thank you, Mr. Hesketh,' said Angela. 'I try to avoid shooting people as a rule, but sometimes one has no choice in the matter. I am only glad I happened to be on the spot today, or who knows what might have happened?'

She left Hesketh to his work and went upstairs to pack her things, for she was to leave the next morning. Given the events, very little work had got done that day by the school as a whole, and most of the teachers had judged it best to give the girls a little freedom, for they knew it was useless to try and make them work. Everyone knew that a man had been killed and that the girl they had known as Irina Ivanoveti had been shot and gravely wounded, and all wanted to talk and wonder over it. The teachers, too, spent much of the time muttering in corners together. They had been given only incomplete information, and they were dying to ask Mrs. Marchmont or Mr. Hesketh what had happened. Neither of them seemed inclined to satisfy anybody's curiosity, however, and so the teachers were forced to be content with the little news they had, until such time as Miss Bell saw fit to explain the situation.

The next morning, Angela went to take her leave of Miss Bell. Now that the danger was over and the miscreants safely out of the way, the headmistress was starting to breathe more easily. Girls and Maths and discipline and teachers she knew and could manage with admirable competence, but international intrigue was quite beyond her and unsettled her severely. Secretly, she was quite relieved that she was shortly to lose the two Moranian girls who had caused her so much trouble, although she would never have admitted the fact. She was also looking forward to the departure of Mrs. Marchmont, who had become associated in her mind—justly or not—with the whole sorry affair.

'Oh, Mrs. Marchmont,' she said, when Angela made her appearance. 'I am just writing an advertisement for a new Latin master. Now that the danger has passed Mr. Hesketh will, of course, be leaving us. It is a great pity, for he is really a very gifted teacher, and I half-thought I might be able to persuade him to take the post permanently. It was not to be, however, and so I must find another one.'

Angela expressed her sympathy and hoped that Miss Bell would be successful in her search.

'Still,' went on Miss Bell, 'at least I do not have to look for a new gardener. It appears that Miss Fazackerley's brother is without a position, and is more than happy to start immediately.'

'Oh?' said Angela, surprised.

'Yes,' said Miss Bell. 'He has had misfortunes in life, and has not always acted for the best, but here at Wakeley Court we are always prepared to give a man the opportunity to improve his lot and his character if he, in turn, is willing to prove his worth. Miss Fazackerley speaks for him and has given assurances of his future good behaviour. Of course, we shall take him on trial to start with, but I very much hope that he will suit.'

'That is good news,' said Angela.

And indeed it was, she thought, as she left Miss Bell's study. Dick Fazackerley had been dragged into the thing when he was in fact wholly innocent. It was pleasant to think that he would now have the chance to prove himself in an honest job.

Morning break-time had arrived, and Angela found Barbara, Florrie and Violet in the Quad, apparently cramming for a Maths test but in reality doing nothing of the sort. Florrie looked quite recovered from her ordeal of the day before, and had refused absolutely to spend a second day in the San.

'Hallo, Angela,' said Barbara. 'Are you really going, then?'

'I am,' said Angela. 'I have just come to say goodbye.'

'You are coming back at the end of the month, though, as you said, aren't you?'

'Yes, I shall be back then,' said Angela, who was determined to keep to her resolution of spending more time with her god-daughter—at least until the Ellises got back from India.

'Then I won't see you again,' said Florrie. 'I'm going back to Morania in the next few days.'

'Are you leaving Wakeley Court for good?' said Angela.

'Perhaps. I don't know,' said Florrie. 'It all depends on how quickly my father gets better. I should like to come back, perhaps for the summer term, but I don't know whether he'll let me.'

'Of course he will, you ass,' said Barbara. 'He can't keep you shut up in a palace forever, can he?'

'"You ass?"' repeated Florrie, sticking her nose in the air haughtily. 'You're not supposed to say that to a princess, you know.'

'Aren't I?' said Barbara. 'I thought it was Moranian for "Your Highness."'

The three girls collapsed in giggles, and Angela shook her head and walked off. In the entrance-hall she met Mlle. Delacroix.

'So, I hear you have saved us all from a dangerous criminal,' said Mam'selle. 'At least, that is the story that is going around. Nobody tells us teachers anything, you understand, and so we have to listen to stories. Is it true?'

Angela confessed that there was some truth in the rumour, and Mam'selle nodded.

'That was very bold of you,' she said. 'Barbara is also a bold one. You are obviously a great influence on her.'

Angela thought of the betting book and was inwardly forced to admit that the French mistress might be right, although whether it were a good influence or a bad one was doubtful.

'She is a good girl,' went on Mam'selle. 'I think she will do well. If you like, I will keep an eye on her and write to you if I think there is any cause for concern.'

'That would be very kind of you,' said Angela.

'I understand how these things are,' said Mam'selle. 'I am also a godmother, you see.'

'Oh?' said Angela.

'Yes,' went on Mam'selle. 'I have a godson. He is seven years old. He lives in Yorkshire. I do not see him as often as I should like.'

'That is a pity,' said Angela.

'Yes, it is,' said Mam'selle simply. 'Still, it cannot be helped.'

There was a pause as the two women regarded one another, then the bell rang for the end of break, and Mam'selle went off to her next lesson with a wave of her hand. Angela stood for a moment, looking after her, then turned and left the building. It was time to go home.

———

New Releases

If you'd like to receive news of further releases by Clara Benson, you can sign up to my mailing list here: clarabenson.com/newsletter.

Books by Clara Benson

THE ANGELA MARCHMONT MYSTERIES

THE FREDDY PILKINGTON-SOAMES ADVENTURES

SHORT STORIES

Angela's Christmas Adventure

The Man on the Train

A Question of Hats

COLLECTIONS

Angela Marchmont Mysteries Books 1-3

Angela Marchmont Mysteries Books 4-6

Freddy Pilkington-Soames Adventures Books 1-3

HISTORICAL FICTION

In Darkness, Look for Stars (published by Bookouture)

The Stolen Letter (published by Bookouture)

OTHER

The Lucases of Lucas Lodge

Printed in Great Britain
by Amazon

33588376R00138